D178f

FIRST A DREAM

FIRST A DREAM

Maureen Daly

SCHOLASTIC HARDCOVER

Scholastic Inc.
New York

Library of Congress Cataloging-in-Publication Data

Daly, Maureen, 1921–
    First a dream / Maureen Daly.
        p.   cm.
    Summary: When Retta moves with her family to California, she is delighted when her boyfriend Dallas gets a summer job there to be near her, but she soon discovers that true love has other obstacles to surmount.

ISBN 0-590-40846-1

    I. Title.
PZ7.D1713Fi   1990
[Fic] — dc19   89-4186
                                                                           CIP
                                                                            AC

12 11 10 9 8 7 6 5 4 3 2 1   0 1 2 3 4 5/9

Printed in the U.S.A.   37

First Scholastic printing, April 1990

With thoughts of Megan always.
And in memory of the late Perry Cann,
our true and only cowboy.

"Nothing happens unless first a dream."

— *Carl Sandburg*

FIRST A DREAM

Chapter 1

It was half past six in the afternoon on the first Tuesday in June. Dallas Dobson had been with her — in the state of California, at least — for more than ten hours.

She had driven alone to the airport to pick him up. Early mornings were still cool this time of year. But now the afternoon sun was lowering, turning the bleak, distant mountains into exotic peaks dark with flaming pinks and a hot, fireball orange. The earthbound rays sent shards of light burning across the desert sand. Every grain seemed hot, separate, and glistening, like polished crystal quartz.

Henrietta Caldwell was glad to be wearing dark glasses, both to mute the desert brilliance and to hide the tears in her eyes.

Something personal had been said about the two of them before she arrived, hurtful words that Dallas had just repeated to her, a rebuff that was as unexpected to Retta as a single dark cloud in a clear sky.

It was Mrs. Bradley who brought the matter up when Dallas was alone with his employer for the first time. She had walked her new ranch hand around the sprawling layout of Rancho Arabian, introduced him to the horses, and outlined his daily chores. Then she listed for him the rules that would govern his employment and conduct at the ranch that summer. Mrs. Bradley had been unexpectedly firm about rules in regard to his girlfriend.

Retta took a deep breath and tried to calm her thoughts by looking at the peaceful scene around her.

She and Dallas were standing just outside his quarters, a small rustic bunkhouse. They were close enough to catch the dust-sweet waft of pollen and honey as a dozen tiny desert bees worked the petunias and white alyssum in the window box.

Beyond the bunkhouse, near the long horse barn, a tom turkey with grizzled wattles circled a spiny cactus, looking for shade. In a nearby open corral, four big Arabian horses, polished gray hides dark with sweat, stood under the palm-frond roofings, slim, powerful necks arched down, resting motionless in the simmer of late afternoon.

These barns and split-rail fences, the hot acres of sand, all this will be home to him for the next three months, she thought. He had been hired to live and sleep here, take orders from the Bradleys, work at chores most of his waking hours.

He will do that, she thought. Dallas will keep his word. But whenever the rules will let me, I want to be with him. That is what he meant when he wrote to make plans for this summer.

Henrietta reached out to lay her fingers lightly on the back of his hand. "How did the matter come up?" she asked quietly. "*Why* did she say what she did?"

He shrugged. "Mrs. Bradley's the boss. She can say whatever she wants." He squinted into the bright sun. "It wasn't meant to be personal, Retta. Just bunkhouse rules. Why is this so important to you?"

"It's important," she said carefully, her fingers still touching him, "because of what you said in that letter. *You* put the words down on paper, so you must have meant them. I thought that was why you came to California.

" '*It's right that I come where you are,*' " she spoke out, as if reading aloud. " '*My father won't need that operation on his legs, so I have the money I saved. We need this time together, don't we?*'

"Aren't those your words, Dallas? I know they are. You wrote them to me. I can recite that letter by heart."

Folded in its envelope, that letter was in the drawer of the night table next to her bed. It was two pages long, written in a strong hand, as if the writer had hunched over a desk, pressing the urgency of his words into the page.

The postmark was their old hometown of Zenith, Pennsylvania. The letter arrived Air Express to Thirty-nine Palms, California, in the middle of May, two weeks after Henrietta and her family had moved west. The Carter Caldwells left after a six-lane highway had destroyed more than half the woods and meadows of their cherished family farm and sent a roar of interstate traffic and an acrid pall of diesel smoke over the once-tranquil countryside.

That was in the springtime. Only the September before, Retta had seen Dallas Dobson for the first time at Havendale High — a shy, new senior, one year ahead of her but trying, at eighteen, to catch up with a junior math class.

As days went by, she learned he was a loner, a part-time school dropout, a part-time cowboy who had moved to Pennsylvania with his father. The older Dobson was a handsome, hard-drinking man with a short temper, a crippled leg, and a demanding need for his son's care and attention.

From the first, Retta was curious about the newcomer from Texas. He was tall, rangy, with dark good looks, a ragged haircut, and scrubbed but calloused and hard-worked hands. His everyday school uniform was a faded denim shirt and jeans, tan windbreaker, and cracked cowboy boots with a Texas star embossed on each ankle.

For some time, the student was aloof not only with Henrietta but with other classmates. But one morning, Retta stopped to pick up Dobson in her car as he left his job at a horse barn to hitchhike to school. As the reserve between them broke, Dallas began to wait for her each day.

It was he who made the first move toward an important and personal relationship. One chill fall evening, after several hours of studying together at a friend's house, he asked her not to take the regular

6

route home, but to drive with him to a parking spot on a remote country road.

"I need to talk to you," he said. And in the darkness of the car, he had told her, "Henrietta, I think we are going to be more than friends. So there are things you should know about me. Things I want to tell you *myself*."

Dallas Dobson revealed to her then that he was an illegitimate child, that his teenaged mother and his father, Daniel Dobson, had never married. She was a clown, sixteen years old, performing with a small rodeo when Dobson met her. And his father had never married the mother of Dallas's older brother, either, beloved Sam Houston, who had been killed in a motorcyle accident in Texas, the same midnight crash that had left the older Dobson with a damaged leg.

After that, as a young teenager, Dallas had tended his father through a period of recovery, kept house in motels and trailers, worked for money to live on, and missed months of schooling. He was now at Havendale High, hoping to catch up, hoping to graduate, hoping to get on with his life.

"I want you to know these things, but I never want you to feel sorry for me," Dallas had said.

Retta listened to his words that night and believed them. She believed also that she had found someone important enough to love.

On her final day at Havendale High, she met with him for the last time in the parking lot of the school. The next day, they both knew, she would be in California, three thousand miles away. The Caldwells had lost not only the home and land they loved so much, but much of their money. And now, Henrietta felt sure, she was about to lose Dallas Dobson.

A second parting would be too difficult. Retta had asked him not to come to the Philadelphia airport to say good-bye.

During the first two weeks in California, Henrietta heard nothing at all from Dallas. Something in her heart made Retta want him to be the one to get in touch. She wanted him to write the first letter, make the first phone call. She longed to know how he felt about their separation, what words he would choose to tell her. There was only silence.

In those strange, empty fourteen days, she became convinced she would *never* hear from him. When she tried to conjure up a memory, she could see almost all of him, the tall body, big shoulders, dark hair, but she could not lure his face into the picture. Their time together in the last months — phone calls, prom night, the long rides in the countryside — seemed also to fade from memory, becoming almost a dream. Then one morning, out of that silence, his letter arrived.

Retta read the pages a dozen times that day, until the words were engraved in her memory and she could see them against her closed eyelids in the nighttime shadows of her room.

"I've done some important thinking since you left," Dallas had written, *"and I want you to know about it.*

"First, I finally talked with my father. I told him I knew he could walk on his bad leg if he wanted to. I told him I had seen him in his room one night through an upstairs window. He was walking like

a normal man, without crutches or a cane. I said I knew his leg had healed a long time ago. And that he was faking the permanent injury to make sure I stayed around.

"I explained that I hadn't talked to you about this, just made up my own mind. I'd decided to go to California for the summer.

"He felt like punching me out, or going into town to buy a bottle, I could tell that. But he didn't. Instead we talked, Retta, like people, like friends even. It was hard for me to find the words, but I said that wherever I was, I'd still love him. I told him how much it meant to me that he kept me when my mother wanted to give me up for adoption. How glad I was he never gave me away to be someone else's kid.

"He promised to get his act together and I believe him. It's right that I come where you are. . . . We need this time together, don't we?

"Second (this is so important and I need your help), I got hold of a copy of Arabian Horse Times. There was an ad in the classifieds. A ranch between Palm Springs and Indio is looking for summer help. I called the number and talked to a Mr. Bradley at Rancho Arabian. He and his wife own the place. I told them what I know about horse care and how much I wanted the job. But they didn't want to hire me over the phone. So I told them about you. Can you drive out to Rancho Arabian and pin down the work for me, let them interview you about me? Try to get me that job, Retta. It will give me wages and a place to live. The ranch is listed in the phone book.

"I'll have to be back in the fall to finish up and

graduate, but if I get the job, we can have almost three months together. I could leave here on June 3rd, that's the first Tuesday in the month.

"When that plane circles over the desert, I dream I'll see your little yellow car coming to meet me."

He had not signed the letter "love" but, *"I'll say it when I see you. Believe me."*

Henrietta Caldwell was awake before six that Tuesday morning. Slatted bedroom shades were drawn, but already slits of daylight showed along the windowsill and laid stripes of brightness on the green carpet.

The plane from Philadelphia was scheduled to land at Palm Springs at eight o'clock. It was a half hour drive from Thirty-nine Palms, but Retta was determined not only to be on time but early.

Yet she wanted to be still for a few minutes more. Resolutely, she lay with her arms at her sides, breathing deeply and evenly, eyes fixed on the ceiling. In those drowsing, waking moments, she was acutely aware of her physical self. She sensed the thin silkiness of her nightgown, the restless warmth of her body. She was aware too of her own fragrant aura, a slight but stirring mix of clean sheets, bath powder, last night's shampoo, and the fruity tropical residue of suntan oil.

Henrietta remembered reading once, back in grade school, that the French queen Marie Antoinette perfumed her rooms in the Versailles palace by waving the cologne-scented fan through burning candle flames.

It was more than three weeks, twenty-two days exactly, since she had said good-bye to Dallas in the parking lot outside the high school; an eternity. Yet today he would be here.

At that moment, lying in bed thinking of Dallas, mingled scents seemed to be everywhere, as if someone had brought fresh flowers into the room. Retta realized that in the joy of the morning, with its warmth and anticipation, she had become her own incandescence, her own candle.

She decided to skip a shower. The sound of running water might wake her brother, Two, and he would ask to ride along. Instead, she knotted a towel around her body like a sarong and went out to the pool.

In the walled garden, nothing moved but the tiny gloss-green leaves on the new lime tree, touched by a breeze so light that Retta could barely feel it.

Dropping the towel, she stepped into the pool, then slipped into the water with hardly a break on the smooth surface. She moved her arms lightly, quietly, watching and feeling the liquid caress of water as it made silver bracelets around her wrists.

If I stay here for a while, she thought, a half hour, no more than that, I will feel cool and clean and there will be less than an hour to wait for him. . . .

Chapter
2

A t the Palm Springs airport, Retta pulled her yellow Volkswagen onto the far side of the parking lot away from the Mercedes-Benzes, BMW's, sports cars, and hotel vans lined up near the main gate. A Rolls-Royce Silver Cloud was parked nearby, a uniformed chauffeur sitting behind the wheel. The car had been positioned carefully under a small palm tree, which cast protective frond shadows across the gleaming radiator and front grill. In the desert light, the distinctive Rolls hood ornament shone like a polished jewel.

Retta parked her car so that it stood alone in the open sunlight, bright enough — she hoped — to be seen from the air. *"I dream I see your little yellow car . . ."* his letter had said.

The Palm Springs airport had been built some years earlier when the town was smaller and air traffic lighter. Now, with resort hotels and luxury condo complexes crowding the desert everywhere with golf courses, green grass, and blue pools, and with "instant towns" such as Thirty-nine Palms springing up, the airport was busy from the first arriving plane at eight o'clock in the morning till the last departure at eight at night.

The arrival board at the United Airlines counter showed that Flight 209 from Philadelphia was a quarter of an hour late. It was now scheduled to land at Runway 2, Gate 1, at fifteen minutes past the hour. Retta felt an unreasonable stab of disappointment. Eight o'clock had seemed so near, eight-fifteen was still so far.

She bought coffee from a vending machine and walked through tinted glass doors toward Runway 2. Standing in the shade, she sipped the hot coffee slowly, determined to make it last until Flight 209 was approaching the tarmac.

Because each incoming flight must make a deep, fast descent from over the high mountains to the landing field, one could hear and feel the vibrations of the powerful engines before the plane itself showed up as a silver flash on the horizon, just over the rim of the San Jacintos. When she felt that noise, Retta finished the coffee in a single swallow, threw the container into a trash bin, and ran quick fingers through her short hair.

The plane made its careful descent, settled like a fat, shining bird on the runway, then taxied to a stop. Uniformed airport workers pushed a flight of movable stairs toward the plane's exit door. Others

13

drove motorized luggage carts to the belly of the plane. An airline stewardess was the first to exit the carrier, standing at the top of the stairs to aid passengers.

Dallas Dobson was not the second person to leave the plane, nor the third nor the fourth. After two-score-more passengers had emerged, blinking in the sunlight, he was still nowhere in sight.

Then she saw him as he ducked to avoid the low doorway, stopping to say something to the stewardess. Retta watched as he hefted a large brown paper shopping bag dangling from one wrist. In each of his hands he carried cat travel cases.

She jumped up and down twice to attract his attention, then waved frantically, but he didn't seem to notice her. She couldn't be sure. At this distance, she could see everything about him — dark hair, tight jeans, the tan windbreaker he'd worn all during the school year — everything but the expression on his face and the look in his eyes. Another figure stepped from the plane and stood with Dallas and the stewardess.

By squinting her eyes, Henrietta could see that Dallas was talking and smiling, but he was not waving toward where she stood, he was not shading his eyes against the sun to look for her. In fact, he seemed to be with someone else.

As the two people neared her, Retta stared intently at the person walking so close to Dallas. She felt she knew her from somewhere. The woman's face was tan as a walnut, her copper-colored hair skinned back and worn in a single, long braid. The slight, wiry body was trim in a beige pants suit worn with a matching hat and slim alligator boots.

It wasn't until the lady turned from Dallas that Retta recognized Gemma Moore, the one-time movie actress now famous for her TV car commercials.

It was Dallas who called out, "Retta!" but it was Gemma Moore who managed to reach her first, linking her arm through Retta's, saying, "I'd have known you anywhere from his description. Don't you think I'm sweet to bring your big guy home to you?"

Retta tried to separate from Miss Moore, but she felt the linked arm tighten ever so slightly. The three moved toward the luggage carousel together, Gemma Moore in the middle, Dallas holding the two cat cages out in front of him, his knees knocking the heavy cages as he walked.

"I don't think I've ever had such an amusing flight," the actress said to Retta. "At first when this big hunk sat next to me, I thought he was just another hungry cowboy. But I found out he was something different, a real gentleman."

"The airline overbooked on tourist-class tickets," Dallas said, "so in Philadelphia they bumped me up to first class and — "

Before Retta could speak, Miss Moore broke in, her lips in a mock pout. "Don't say silly things like that, Dallas. You *are* first class. Even the cats liked you right away." She turned to Retta. "I never travel anywhere without my babies."

The carousel was already turning with luggage from Flight 209. A chauffeur, the one Retta had seen in the Rolls, stepped forward to say, "I've already got your bag, Miss Moore. It must have been the first one off. And the car is out front."

15

"Oh, Dominic, you're too efficient," she said. "But we're staying right here until my friend's luggage comes round. We're going to drop these young people wherever they want to go."

"Oh, please don't wait for us, Miss Moore," Retta said quickly. "I have my car."

"Oh, bother," the woman said with some irritation. "I'm always having my good times spoiled." She turned to the chauffeur. "Take the cats, Dominic. I'll be right out."

When Dallas handed over the carrying cases, Gemma Moore stepped in front of him and reached both hands to his shoulders. He bent down and turned his face slightly so her kiss landed on his cheek. She touched the spot lightly and said, "There. Now you've been kissed by a star. Don't wash that off till next Christmas. You have my Hollywood phone number, Dallas. Let me know when you have some time off. I can't bear to think of you sweating out the summer all alone on some back-road ranch."

"Rancho Arabian is a great place," Retta said defensively. "Beautiful, in fact."

"Oh, don't worry yourself, sweetheart," Miss Moore said. "Your boyfriend didn't give me a map to the old homestead. And he didn't tell me that you were such a tiger princess, either. Or don't you know that yet, Dallas?"

She was looking directly at Retta, standing so close that Henrietta could see the sunburned grain of the woman's skin, the fine, threadlike wrinkles at the corners of her eyes. "I don't think you'll *let* him call me, will you?" she said.

"I can walk you to your car, if that's what you'd

like, ma'am," Dallas said hurriedly. "I certainly appreciated your company today." But she didn't seem to hear him. She was still looking at Retta, assessing her, as if trying to analyze something elusive she could not understand in the younger woman's face or manner.

Finally, she said, "Sixteen years old, or seventeen, aren't you? And all excited about your first man. Sweet, but not very realistic, I'm afraid. No, I was never that young, Retta — or that confident. And I wouldn't want to be."

Gemma Moore gave Dallas a last pat on the cheek and walked toward one of the exit doors. "Don't be hard on her," he said quietly to Retta. "I think she's a nice lady, but she's had a lot of champagne."

"Champagne?"

He nodded. "You get a champagne breakfast in first class. Miss Moore was awake and talking, so they started serving her somewhere over Colorado. I wasn't having champagne, so she drank mine. She's just lonely, I guess."

For the next few moments, neither spoke. When his worn duffel bag finally appeared on the carousel, Dallas shifted the paper shopping sack to his left hand and swung the duffel bag over one shoulder with his right. "That's it, Retta," he said. "I'm here."

"My car is in the parking lot," she said. "I parked it to one side, off by itself. Could you see it, Dallas, looking down from the plane?"

He paused, then said, "I've got to be honest with you, Henrietta. I forgot to look."

Outside the tinted glass doors of the terminal building, Dallas stopped, squinting his eyes at the bright sunshine and the clear blue sky. Retta looked around slowly, trying to make herself comprehend just what he was seeing for the first time, the masses of flowers, a big, bubbling decorative fountain, lines of expensive cars and resort limos with glistening chrome, people with deep tans in pastel golf or tennis outfits.

Dallas rubbed his hand over his eyes. "Never saw a day as bright as this one," he said. "Not even in Texas."

"You'll need to buy yourself good sunglasses," Retta said. "Everyone out here wears them."

He shook his head. "Not for me. You never see a cowhand or a real horseman in sunglasses. It would be a kind of city-type thing to do. I'll just have to get used to it."

Then *don't* buy sunglasses, she thought, with an irrelevant surge of anger. *Give* your champagne to strangers if you want. Just *ruin* your stubborn cowboy eyes if that's what you want to do.

They walked wordlessly across the parking lot, the black pavement already reflecting the growing heat of the sun. When they got to the yellow car, Dallas slung his duffel bag into the backseat, then slid into the front passenger side, just as he had so often in Pennsylvania, pulling his long legs so his knees rested against the dashboard. He placed the shopping bag on the floor between them. Retta looked down and read the logo: "Crossroads General Store." Dallas caught her glance.

He waited till she backed out of the parking place and proceeded toward the exit. "I didn't expect to come traveling with my stuff in a paper bag," he said.

"It doesn't matter," Retta said quickly.

"You were staring at it in the airport. And you looked at it again right now," he said. "Let me tell you what happened.

"Last night I finished up late at the Kennelly barn. I needed extra socks and shorts, so I drove to the General Store. When I got home, my father was asleep. At least his door was locked. I couldn't borrow his luggage."

Retta felt a clutch of apprehension. "He didn't take you to the airport? You told me he wasn't going to drink anymore."

"Maybe he was just tired," he said. "Junior Provanza and your friend Charlie drove me."

"I can't believe your father wouldn't want to take you to the airport to say a real good-bye," she said. Even as she heard her own words, she wished fervently that she had not spoken her thoughts aloud.

The silence that followed was so lengthy, so pronounced, that Retta finally said, "Turn on the radio if you want, Dallas. We can listen to some music."

He turned the dial, catching snatches of voices singing against guitar backgrounds. "Only country and western?" he said.

"Either that or golden oldies for the golf crowd," she said. He settled for something by Johnny Cash and turned the sound down low.

"I can't explain my father, Retta," he said. "You knew that back in Pennsylvania. Still, *not* saying good-bye is a way of *saying* good-bye. He had to make that decision. At least he was thinking of me."

Dallas pointed to the dashboard clock. "Is that the right time?"

"Not quite," she said. "I keep it about five minutes fast."

"And how long is the ride to Rancho Arabian?"

"About twenty minutes more," she said. "It's about a quarter to nine now. I thought we'd stop somewhere for breakfast . . . " she said eagerly.

"I ate breakfast on the plane," he said. "I just didn't drink the champagne."

Retta spoke quickly, determined to keep this new disappointment out of her voice. "That's all right, Dallas," she said brightly. "I can have something at home while you say hello to my parents. I want to show you the new house and — "

Dallas stared out the side window, then cleared his throat before interrupting. "That will have to wait, Retta. I've got to get to work. Mrs. Bradley phoned me a couple of days ago to know when my plane got in. Mr. Bradley's a lawyer as well as a horse breeder. He has to fly to Miami this morning. She wants me to meet him first. Their regular horse man left for Europe a couple of days ago. He's going to work with Polish Arabians for the summer, you know. The Bradleys are counting on me this morning."

Retta's hand tightened involuntarily on the steering wheel. "But right from the plane? Didn't Mrs. Bradley think that — "

"Right from the plane," he cut in. "With that fifteen-minute delay in arrival, I'm already about to be late."

"All right, Dallas," she said, "I know a shortcut."

At the next traffic light, she moved into a left-hand-turn lane and waited till she could slip in amid a line of pickup trucks, heavy gasoline tankers, and flatbeds loaded with crates of produce. Even though the traffic was almost bumper to bumper, the air oily with diesel fumes, it moved rapidly. After a few miles the vehicles began to thin out as the highway wended off into open country — stretches of rough, rocky sands with only a few scattered buildings in sight.

Finally, from the main highway, Retta turned off onto a narrow, partially paved road laced with fissures from the summer heat and winter frost of the harsh desert climate.

For several miles, Dallas had sat without speaking, his big hands motionless on his knees, his mood so withdrawn that his silence seemed to accentuate the noise of the flying gravel hitting the fenders and underside of the Volkswagen.

The car was now approaching a fifty-foot stretch of towering tamarisks lining one side of the road, the trees planted so close together that the long, feathery branches and fine, needlelike leaves intertwined and meshed together into a thick green wall.

"This is it," she said, once more forcing her voice to sound relaxed. "These trees mark the beginning of the Rancho Arabian property. Old-time ranchers used to plant tamarisks as windbreaks. Up ahead, at the end of these trees, I'll make a left turn. Then you can see the Bradleys' two hundred acres."

"You mean we're almost there?" he said.

"Yes. We made good time."

He looked at the dashboard clock and then put his hand on the steering wheel. "Pull over, Retta," he said.

"Where? What do you mean?"

"I want you to pull over right here," he said, point-

21

ing to the narrow shoulder of road. "I want to talk to you." Retta glanced out the side window. They were almost halfway along the big windbreak. "This is a public road," she said. "I can't just pull over and park wherever I choose."

"Yes, you can. Please don't argue. Just pull over."

"I could get stuck in the sand."

"Then you get out and I'll pull the car over."

"All right," she said. "I'll try." She rolled down the window and examined the roadway. If she was careful, she judged, there was just enough flinty gravel to make a firm parking spot tight against the big hedge.

When she turned off the motor and rolled up the driver's window, she was aware that the small car was half nestled in the low, dusty branches of the trees.

Ahead of them and to the right, the countryside was still a bright, sharded glitter in the morning sunlight, but the car itself was partially hidden in a cocoon of shadow.

I'm not going to let myself cry, she thought desperately. Even if he wants to drive up to Hollywood, or if he's decided to take the next plane back to Philadelphia. If this trip was a mistake, we should both admit it now. . . .

"Henrietta, look at me!"

She was aware that she might cry, so she looked ahead through the windshield. "I can hear you without looking at you, Dallas."

He put both hands lightly on her shoulders to turn her toward him, but, almost involuntarily, she resisted. He tightened his grip, forcing her to turn.

22

She gasped sharply, shaken by the sudden nearness of his face.

"I didn't mean to hurt you," he said.

"You didn't. I think I was more surprised."

For a moment he hesitated, then drew a finger along the arch of each of her eyebrows. She smelled the lilac-sweet scent of airline soap and reacted to the warmth of his fingertips.

"What are we doing, Henrietta?" he asked. "What's happening?"

At the softness of his words, she longed to reach out to him, but confusion stopped her. Instead, she heard herself begin to speak, words tumbling out erratically. "What's happening," she said, "is that everything is all wrong between us. That's what's happening." She paused for a breath.

"You flew in from Philadelphia this morning, and I just couldn't *wait* for you to land. You wrote you'd hoped to see my car when you flew in, but you forgot to look. I waved when you got off the plane, but you couldn't wave because you were carrying two cats and talking to some woman who drank all your champagne. I wanted to stop somewhere to have a chance to talk to you, just to *look* at you, but Mrs. Bradley has you on a deadline. . . ."

Dallas didn't answer, but instead put one hand on her shoulder, moving it so he could brush through her hair with his fingertips.

"And more important than all that," she continued, her voice faltering, "the really awful thing is that we're sitting here, embarrassed to be alone together. We have nothing to say. . . ."

He shook his head. "You're not helping, Retta."

"And neither are you," she said, her voice husky. "You weren't glad to see me when you got off the plane. You wanted to do favors and talk to that other person. I think you blame me because we've got sunlight and sand in California instead of all that green stuff growing back in Pennsylvania. You can't even say something good about *sunglasses*, for goodness' sake!"

She felt his hand warm and insistent on the nape of her neck, pressing her toward him. "Please, Dallas," she said unsteadily. "Don't do that. You're making me nervous. I feel almost like I'm sitting next to a stranger. . . ."

He drew away, took his arm from her shoulder, folded his hands on his knees, and looked straight ahead.

"I don't think you should talk anymore, Retta. At least not right now."

"Fine," she said, "I don't want to talk, either."

She turned the car key and, without looking over her shoulder, shifted rapidly into reverse. The automobile lurched backward abruptly, then stalled as the tires spun in the loose sand. Before she could change gears, Dallas leaned forward with easy deliberation and turned the ignition key, shutting off the motor.

"We're not going anywhere," he said. "At least not right away. I don't want you running into some fence post just to prove how mad at me you are."

"Please. I really don't want to talk anymore," Retta said.

"You don't have to, Retta. I think it's my turn." He paused a moment, frowning. "I'm not sure what went wrong, and it doesn't really matter. I don't want

24

to argue about it. I want to get back to where we were in Pennsylvania," he said. "We've got a problem right now we can't solve unless we're friends. If we can't communicate with words, we should communicate in whatever way we can. I'm sure of that."

At this moment it was he who made no attempt to look at her, to give her the encouragement of his eyes.

"But I'm afraid of something, Retta. I'm afraid that if you don't kiss me this morning, right here in this car — I don't believe you will ever kiss me again. And that means that I can never kiss you. I don't like to think about that."

He was gazing out into the desert morning, letting her consider her response, his hands still gripped loosely on his knees. It was a waiting silence.

Looking over at him in the shadows of the tamarisks, she became aware of something she had almost forgotten — the semicircular burn on his left hand, a healing scar, white as a half-moon against the dark skin.

The scar reminded her vividly of the morning last year when she saw that hurt and battered hand for the first time. With the memory came a rush of emotion and the sting of real tears to her eyes.

It had been cold that day when she stopped at the Kennellys' barn to pick him up for school. He was without gloves, shivering, and the back of his hand was marked with a deep, raw burn.

Dallas told her that morning, sitting in the same yellow car, that in a drunken spell of self-pity the night before, his father had gathered together all the pictures of his dead son, Sam Houston Dobson,

25

some of his clothing and books, even the sheet music for his guitar, and thrown it all into the lit fireplace in that shabby old house on Snuff Mill Road.

"I put my hand in the fire for my brother," he said. "I pulled out his clothes, his music, because I didn't want to lose that part of him, the things he'd touched. It can't be right not to remember, Retta, to pretend such a great guy never was."

It had been that intensity, the words of loyalty and caring on a cold Pennsylvania day, that made Retta recognize for the first time Dallas Dobson's deep determination and his capacity for love.

She remembered how desperately she had wanted to touch his raw, burned hand that morning, to kiss some joy into the face so withdrawn and haunted. Those things, she realized now, were what she wanted still.

"I need a few moments to be with myself," she whispered, barely loud enough to be heard. She reached over to lay her hand on his, feeling the silk of that old, smooth scar tissue under her fingertips.

"I *want* to kiss you, Dallas," she said. "But I feel like I forgot how."

He turned toward her and said, "I can show you, Retta. Trust me. You'll remember."

Mrs. Bradley was in the driveway, putting mail into the box for the postman, when the yellow car turned in the gates. Retta saw her glance at her wristwatch, but the woman smiled when the two young people got out of the car.

"Good morning, Henrietta," she said, then put out her hand. "We're glad to have you here, Dallas Dobson. Mr. Bradley is in the house with our son, Burton, interviewing a teacher. Burton didn't do too well in ninth grade this year. We plan to have him stay at our place in Scottsdale for tutoring most of the summer."

"I'll be pleased to meet your family, ma'am," Dallas said.

"Good. But first I'll show you your quarters and help you get acquainted with the ranch." She smiled at Retta. "You're looking sweet, my dear. Like girls I went to college with in New England, very eastern."

Retta was aware of her windblown hair and wrinkled skirt, the touches of perspiration on her cotton blouse. "I haven't done much California shopping yet," she said.

"We're pretty much a blue jeans crowd at Rancho Arabian," Mrs. Bradley said. "I find the work gets done better that way."

She turned to Dallas. "Have you had breakfast? Would you like to wash up and rest for an hour or so?"

"No, thanks, ma'am. There was breakfast on the plane. I'm ready to work."

Mrs. Bradley put a tanned, well-manicured hand on Retta's shoulder. "We'll get along just fine, your young man and I. The pickup truck, the one Dallas will be using, gets back from the garage tomorrow. So why don't you drive out here around six this evening? Dallas will be free."

"I'd rather put in some good work hours before I take time off, Mrs. Bradley," he said.

"Oh, you will," she answered lightly. "I'll tell you about that, and other things you'll need to know so you can do the kind of job we want here. We don't have many rules at Rancho Arabian, but the rules we *do* have, my husband and I expect you to abide by."

When Henrietta moved her car to the end of the drive, she rolled down a window and looked back through the dust to wave good-bye. Dallas had already put his duffel bag and paper sack to one side, and he and his new employer were walking away from her, toward the barn.

Chapter
3

A t Desert Lily Street, Retta's mother's car was in
the garage but Carter Caldwell's slot was empty.

Once inside the quiet house, Retta noticed that
the terrace table had been set for five, with a cof-
feepot on a warmer and a bowl of fresh fruit resting
in ice. Connie Caldwell was stretched beside the
pool, her face turned up to the sun.

"I should have phoned before you went to this
trouble, Mother," Retta called out. "He won't be here
for breakfast. . . ."

Mrs. Caldwell sat up and blinked her eyes. "Don't
worry about it, Retta. Your father just had some
coffee and went to the office. Two is off somewhere
with his pals. Just put the fruit in the refrigerator,
will you?"

Retta brought the fruit into the kitchen, then switched it from the crystal bowl to a plastic container, grateful for the few moments alone. She knew her mother would want to talk about Dallas, but Retta needed a respite. The intensity of those minutes beside the tamarisk trees was too personal to articulate to anyone.

Her mother came into the kitchen just then, wearing a sundress and matching jacket that covered her bare shoulders. A red leather briefcase swung from her wrist.

"So, Henrietta," her mother said. "How's Dallas?"

"I'm going to drive out to Rancho Arabian to see him at six this evening," Retta responded quickly, aware she was not answering her mother's question. "Mrs. Bradley suggested it. And he's taller than I remember," she added. "Or maybe it's just the tight jeans."

"How did he get to the airport?" Mrs. Caldwell asked.

"Junior Provanza drove him. His father had to work, I guess," she said defensively.

"Mr. Dobson was working? I didn't know feed and grain stores were open at night."

"Mother, how can I possibly know all these details when Dallas has been here no more than two hours?" She tried to quiet the tremor in her voice. "Mrs. Bradley put him right to work. I've barely had a chance to talk to him."

"I know, I know," her mother said quickly. "I just wondered if he's happy to be in California."

Retta shrugged. "I think so. Except for Pennsylvania and sort of bumming around Texas as a young person, Dallas hasn't been many places. . . . He

30

didn't bring much luggage, either. Just a duffel bag and some loose things in a paper sack." Retta paused.

She became aware that her mother was looking at her intently, concentrating, yet distracted. "An ordinary paper sack?" her mother said. "I hope you didn't embarrass him. I mean, what's so wrong with a paper bag?"

Abruptly, Mrs. Caldwell pulled car keys from her briefcase and said, "If I'm going to do an editorial about those developers and the old date plantations, I'd better go take a look."

At the back door, she paused. "Your father wants you to stop by the newspaper at eleven. He has a plan he needs to talk over with you."

The phone in the front hall rang. Mrs. Caldwell opened the outside door saying, "That must be the Save the Trees group. Tell them I'm on my way, will you?"

Retta hurried to the phone. But it was not a member of the committee after all. It was Charlotte Amberson, Jr., calling from Zenith, Pennsylvania. The call was for Henrietta Caldwell, person-to-person and collect.

The voice was breathless, conspiratorial. "Tell me, Retta. How's the cowboy?"

Charlotte Amberson had been her friend, almost like a sister, back in Zenith. Most of their lives the girls had lived just a few miles apart, Henrietta with her family in a big, stone house and Charlotte with her divorced mother in a small, rented brick house at the side of a country lane.

Now her friend's tone was impatient. "What was

31

the very first thing he said to you, when you were alone, when you got where *nobody else could hear?*"

Retta moved across the foyer, letting the long phone cord trail behind her. She kicked off her thong sandals and stepped carefully into a banded pattern of sunlight that lay on the floor, slanting through the bamboo blinds. The ribbons of light fell warm and sensuous across her ankles.

"Why are you so quiet, Retta?" Charlotte's question was shrill. "What did you and the cowboy *say* to each other?"

Retta chose her words carefully. "I *believe* the first thing I said was, 'Dallas Dobson, old sport, your plane is late. That means that you are late and if you don't hump leather right out to the Bradley place, you're gonna get fired the first day and — ' "

"All right, Retta." Charlotte's voice was sharp with disappointment. "You don't even talk that way. Keep all the good stuff to yourself if you want. You just don't know how *nothing* life is for *me* right now."

"What do you mean, Charlie? What's the matter?"

"We're going flat broke, that's what's the matter. We can't pay our bills. Mother hasn't had a job since your parents closed the paper here and zapped her column. We've been eating plum pudding all week, some canned stuff somebody sent from London a couple of years ago."

"Plum pudding?" Retta said. "Remember when Aunt Blue worked for us? After Christmas, she liked to fry leftover slices. We'd eat it for breakfast with honey."

"But did you ever try eating it *cold*, Henny, and

three nights in a row? Besides," she said, "your Aunt Blue was a super cook. Remember the blueberry cake she made for us the day you elected her something?"

Retta's thoughts warmed at the memory. It seemed so long ago, that afternoon when she was only six or seven, and she had told Aunt Blue that she wanted her for a grandmother. They'd been sitting in the Caldwell kitchen, Aunt Blue reading her Bible, the fields outside white with snow.

"You're a sweet child to say that," Aunt Blue had told her. "But you got actual *kinfolk* to love you. I know your mama's mama is dead, God keep her, but you've got a perfectly good grandmother living down in Florida that you haven't half used up yet."

"But I like you best, Aunt Blue," Retta had said.

"We don't need 'bests' or 'betters' in this house," the old black woman had answered tartly. "We're all God's people, square and even."

"If you can't be my real grandmother, I'll make you an honorary grandmother, Two's and mine," young Henrietta insisted. "I can do that whether you say so or not, Aunt Blue."

It was then the old lady suggested they make a blueberry cake together. "Get your brother, and call your friend to bicycle over," she said. "We all got something to celebrate."

Charlotte's unhappy voice jarred Retta back to the present. "Aren't you even *listening* to me out there?"

"Of course I am. I just didn't know things were so bad with you. Couldn't *you* find some kind of summer work?"

"I tried. Junior promised me a job as a bagger at

33

their store weekends. He even said he'd pick me up and drop me off, but Mother vetoed the whole thing."

"But if you have bills, Charlie . . . A bagger's job could pay six dollars an hour."

"I know that. But Mother doesn't want me to go out with a boyfriend who is a part-time butcher, even if he works for his father. She'd rather sell my bike, the electric lawn mower, even her Glenn Miller record collection. She did that this week."

"Don't you still get money from your father?"

"No," Charlotte said. "Child support got cut off when I turned seventeen. There hasn't been any alimony for Mother, either, since she married that third guy."

Charlie interrupted herself sharply. "Why are we talking about *me?* Even if you're paying for it, this *is* my phone call. I want you to tell me about you and Dallas. I'm still your best friend, aren't I?"

Retta thought quickly. She knew Charlotte well. She was a generous and loyal person, but with inner feelings as fragile and breakable as a speckled egg at the edge of a nest.

"Listen, Charlie," she said. "Right now, I'm supposed to be on my way to the newspaper. I'll write or call you this week. I promise."

"You'd *better*," her friend said with a high, nervous laugh. "Otherwise I'll never get the chance to tell you what Dallas and his father had that big fight about just before he left."

"What are you saying? *What* fight?"

"You wouldn't want to know, Retta. Then we'd be talking about your boyfriend and you just told me you don't have time for that kind of conversation. . . ."

"Charlotte!" Retta said totally interested now. "You can't bring up a subject like that and just drop it!"

"It was meant to be a joke, sort of." Charlotte was suddenly contrite. "It just slipped out. Junior made me promise not to tell." There was an awkward pause. "Henny, I didn't mean to do this. I better hang up before I say anything else."

"Wait! Just give me — " but Charlotte had hung up.

Twice Retta dialed the old brick house in Pennsylvania. She heard a buzzing sound at the other end of the line, but no real ring and no one answered.

It had been a collect call, Retta reminded herself, and Charlie had not said she was calling from home. Perhaps the telephone bill was one of those that had not been paid.

The white adobe structure that housed the *Palms Gazette* newspaper had been erected even more recently than the house on Desert Lily. The building stood at the highway's edge about a half mile out of Thirty-nine Palms. A few knobby oleander cuttings had been planted on two sides of the black macadam parking lot. In a couple of years, the plants would grow to form a tall hedge, green-leafed with pink flowers, but now they were no more than dry, gnarled shafts stuck in the ground.

It was still almost two hours before noontime but already the June heat was climbing. At the moment, a dry warm wind stirred the air and, as Retta walked from her parked car to the front door of the newspaper, she felt the fine grit of sand particles between her teeth.

Carter Caldwell was at work in the editor's office, just off a big open city room arranged with desks, computers, and telephones for a half dozen staffers. Caldwell was checking newspaper page proofs, peering down at the printed columns through blue-tinted glasses. When Retta entered, he pushed the glasses onto his forehead and smiled at her.

"You're early," he said. "I expected you to spend more time with your young man."

"I wanted to, but he's already on the job."

"So soon? He just arrived at eight o'clock, didn't he? I heard your car pull out when you left for the airport." He was looking at his daughter intently, his eyes clouded by a frown.

"Oh, Poppy, don't worry about me," she said quickly. "Dallas is fine, and so am I. Tonight at six I meet him at the ranch. He's got a place of his own behind the big house, kind of a one-man bunkhouse. It probably has a little stove or hot plate. Maybe I'll cook him something. Is there anything else I can tell you?"

Carter Caldwell's face was still thoughtful. "Not unless you want to, Retta, and I guess you don't. So . . . let's talk about your work here."

Retta reacted with surprise. "At the paper? I didn't know you had something for me to do."

"We talked this over a few nights ago, your mother and I," her father continued. "We could use a young viewpoint on the staff right now. I'd like to count

on you for a couple of feature stories a week —
local color, community interest. Once in a while I
might send you to cover a straight story or a social
event."

"Write for the paper? I've only done book reports
and papers for school," Retta said. "Maybe I'm not
good enough for the *Gazette.*"

"We think you are, and I'd like to find out. Your
brother wanted a summer job and went right to the
circulation department. He got hired for a paper
route without even explaining he was my son.

"And besides, Retta, I feel you need something
to occupy your time these next months when your
young man is working."

"But what if I'm not good enough?" Retta said
again. "I wouldn't want you to use my articles if
they're not good, Poppy."

"Don't worry about that," he said sharply. "I won't.
I'll expect your best. I need quality work. Anything
not up to professional standards won't see print."

He took the tinted glasses from his forehead and
laid them on the desk. "Sorry. I didn't mean to snap
at you." He paused. "I'm sure you know the meaning
of the word 'nepotism.' "

"No, I don't," she said, "but I can look it up in
the dictionary."

"I'll tell you," her father said quietly. "Nepotism
is a common practice in many businesses. The word
comes from the Latin, and the roots translate both
as 'nephew' and 'grandson.' It means favoritism,
such as hiring a relative for an important position
because of the relationship rather than merit. This
newspaper isn't run that way."

Retta nodded. "That's why you're so proud of Two for getting himself a job without putting out that he was kinfolk to the boss man."

Her father smiled. "You're trying to sound like Aunt Blue, God bless her."

"Aunt Blue was shrewd about money, too," Henrietta said. "She'd expect me to ask if I'm going to be paid to write for the newspaper."

"Of course," her father said. "For every five-hundred-word story that's good enough to print, we'll pay you thirty-five dollars. That could mean seventy dollars a week for you."

"Shall I start tomorrow?"

"Why not start today? You told me you can't see Dallas till six tonight." Henrietta shrugged, then nodded.

"I have an idea for a feature story I'd like you to look into," Mr. Caldwell said. "I want you to try an article — your personal viewpoint — on what a person can buy for a dollar today in the Desert Mall."

"No one can buy *anything* of value for a dollar these days," she said.

"You just came up with a bright, challenging lead sentence," her father said. "Now drive over to the mall and find out whether you're right or not."

Retta rose from the chair. "I'll give it my best try. But I'd like an advance on my first assignment. Can I have thirty-five dollars now?"

"This is highly irregular, Retta. I expect to pay you as we pay all free-lancers — when the article is completed and okayed for print."

"Come on, Poppy," she said. "A little nepotism, just this once, so I can buy new jeans. I need western pants, tight ones, with studs on the back pockets."

Carter Caldwell counted out three tens and a five from his wallet. "This is an advance, young lady, *not* a loan. And don't go too California. I don't want to see red boots or tattoos, that sort of thing."

Retta put the money in her wallet. "Thank you. First I find the jeans, then I try the story."

"Just make that vice versa, Henrietta," her father said. "And perhaps you'd better look up nepotism in the dictionary after all. I'm not sure you understand exactly what the word means."

The Desert Mall, new as the town of Thirty-nine Palms, was designed to complement its natural surroundings. A two-story building with several broad skylight towers, the whole complex sprawled over several acres and was painted a uniform desert beige. The entire interior, with its dozens of shops and small eating places, was an artificially lit and air-chilled haven protected from the winds, heat, and sand of the desert.

Retta took a deep breath, savoring the fragrances and cool air. The inside fountains and dozens of tubbed trees and flowers were well-tended and re-freshingly real — an eco-culture completely unlike the sand world outside.

Impetuously, she decided to look for a pay phone before starting her assignment. She wanted to talk with Dallas now, and for three reasons: He would be as surprised and excited as she was to hear about her new job; she wanted to learn how his first day was going; but mostly — now that he was so wonderfully nearby — she longed to hear his voice, if only for a few moments.

The correct change was already counted out and

Retta was ready to dial when a thought of caution crossed her mind.

"We don't have many rules at Rancho Arabian," Mrs. Bradley had instructed Dallas that morning, "but the rules we *do* have, both my husband and I expect you to abide by."

Those rules might well include no personal phone calls during working hours, Retta thought, and slipped the coins back into her shoulder bag.

The new jeans came first after all. A blast of country music from a mart called Hell for Leather told Retta this was the boutique to shop in. She paid for her purchase in cash and put the change in her wallet except for one dollar, which went into her skirt pocket.

" . . . *what a person can buy today for a dollar in the Desert Mall,*" that was her assignment.

In a tour of more than a dozen shops, a variety of items caught her attention: Cactus shampoo at ninety-seven cents; magnetic pigs to stick on a refrigerator door, marked down to forty-five cents a pair; imported carrot macaroni at ninety-nine cents a pound; a Taiwanese wooden embroidery hoop for forty-four cents; six shirt buttons on a card for seventy-nine cents; even a wiener-shaped toy dog that smelled like smoked ham, price-tagged at ninety-nine cents.

Nothing seemed exciting or significant enough to write a newspaper article about.

Retta stepped onto the escalator to ride to the shops on the upper level in one of the skylight towers.

Unexpectedly, a voice called out, "Hi, there, Retta!"

She looked up to see her brother riding the opposite "down" escalator just a few yards from her. "What are you doing here anyway?" he called out in raised tones. "Where's the big guy?"

Before she could answer, the moving escalator had carried them both beyond talking distance, so Retta waved and blew a kiss.

A pair of older teenaged boys, tall and sun-blond, stood directly behind Two. The taller of the young men leaned forward and spoke a few words to her brother but she could not make out what was being said. Then that stranger looked up at her and waved his hand, or maybe he blew a kiss. Since he was nearly a full floor beneath her by then, she couldn't tell which.

Retta smiled to herself at this spontaneous friendliness. He's probably got one of those typical California beach-boy names like Lance or Torque or Sandy, she thought. He's probably —

She shook her head with impatience to clear away this sudden, irrelevant daydreaming. At the moment, she felt annoyed with both herself and her brother. Two had always been overly friendly with strangers, willing to talk to just anyone. Perhaps she ought to speak to him about this.

During the second hour of research for her article, Retta began to feel weary, with an ache in her leg muscles from walking on hard terrazzo in flat sandals. The air-conditioning seemed chilly now instead of refreshing, and the constant murmur and movement of the shoppers made her head ache.

Two separate things lured her into a quieter section of the mall: The sound of tumbling water and the smell of fresh coffee. She realized she was both tired and hungry.

With the dollar bill from her pocket, she paid fifty cents for a large peanut butter cookie, then forty-five cents for steaming coffee in a Styrofoam cup. She carried her breakfast to a stone bench near one of the fountains.

The cookie tasted sweet and nutty, the coffee sharply strong. Fragrance from the green leaves and the liquid music of the water were soothing. Retta slipped off her sandals and pressed her feet against the smooth, cool flooring.

As she rested, she became aware of someone sitting at the far end of the bench — an old woman in a worn green dress, thin, wrinkled arms as sharp and angular as a grasshopper. She pretended to be staring ahead, but Retta caught the quick flick of her gaze before she turned away. The woman began to hum softly.

Impulsively, Retta broke the cookie into two parts and held out the larger piece. "I wonder if you'd like this," she said. "And this coffee. I only wanted a sip."

The woman took a small bite from the cookie, then picked up the coffee. "I got nothing to trade with you," she said. "But we could talk. Even if you hadn't spoke up first, I was going to say something. I was going to tell you I remember how it feels to be pretty like you. It don't seem that long ago, either."

"Thank you. That's a nice thing a say."

"I *was* pretty in the old days and I knew how to *work*," the lady said firmly. "That's why it don't hurt to remember."

For the next few minutes, the woman sat savoring the cookie and coffee, and remembering aloud. She had been born on an Oklahoma farm and came west with her family in the Dust Bowl days. As a child, she harvested crops up and down the West Coast, quit school in her teens to marry and start a family, then followed her restless husband to Alaska. When he died there, she raised her twin sons and made a living trapping in fur country. A decade ago, she came back to California to search for her Oklahoma family, but everyone was gone now. Her home was in a trailer in a campground nearby. And she spent every day but Sunday in the cool, green mall.

"Sunday's still the Lord's day and always will be," she said to Retta. "I can still honor Him even if I've got no cool air except a fan."

Retta glanced at her watch just then, startled by the time. She rose from the bench and put out her hand. "I'm glad we could share time," she said. "I'm glad you remember so much."

The old woman wiped her fingers on the green dress and patted Retta's hand, the touch as light and dry as fine paper.

"I *believe* you were pretty, *very* pretty," Retta said.

Back at the *Gazette*, Retta picked a vacant desk as far from the editor's office as possible. She would have preferred to work on this first assignment alone. In the busy city room, the staccato of other machines and the murmur of voices into phones were too professional, too daunting.

The palms of her hands were damp as she put a fresh sheet of paper into the typewriter. Nearly two hours later, she typed out the final version of her article and brought it into her father's office.

"Take a seat," he said. "I've got time to go over your copy now."

"What if I just drive on home, Poppy, and you call me there?" she asked.

"Sit *down*, Henrietta," he said firmly.

She picked one of the new beige armchairs and settled into it self-consciously, a light flush in her cheeks. She waited. Her father seemed to read so slowly. A couple of times he used his pencil. Occasionally his eyes seemed to go over the same paragraph twice.

"I can always try it over again," Retta said, but he raised a silencing hand.

Finally, he laid the pages on his desk. " *'A single dollar buys a lot more in the mall if you have someone to share it with.'* That's a fine last line, Retta."

"Oh, dear. Does that mean you don't like the rest of it?" she asked.

"You've got a couple of dangling participles, and there is only one 'l' in the word 'escalator,' but I've made those corrections."

He took a colored pencil from the desk and wrote a big OK in the margin of the first page. Then he smiled.

"Go see your young man. But remember, I expect a second story from you this week. We'll use the byline 'Henrietta Caldwell' on this one," he added. "It's more professional than a nickname."

Chapter
4

At six that evening, daylight was still everywhere, warm and bright. Just beyond Rancho Arabian, the lowering sun played off scattered white clouds over the mountain peaks so that the stark desert range was dappled with pink and gray shadows.

Dallas was waiting just inside the main gate in fresh jeans and a shirt, a red bandanna knotted around his head, holding back damp hair. The ranch was quiet except for the hum of air-conditioning units and the occasional nickering of horses.

Some distance from the buildings, four elegant Arabians attached to a mechanical exerciser were moving in a circle, kicking up dust as they walked.

"I'm through for today," Dallas said, gesturing around him, "except for these fellows. They need about twenty minutes more on the exerciser. Then I'll towel them down and put them in for the night.

"Mrs. Bradley is here," he added. "I can take some time off the property. If you want to, I mean."

Retta was studying the big exercise contraption. "It looks expensive," she said.

"It is. Everything's up-to-date at this ranch. There's even a TV system with screens and automatic cameras that can cover anywhere inside the barns or in the yards."

"Whatever for?" she asked with interest.

"Part of an overall plan," Dallas explained. "There's a lot of valuable stock here. Mrs. Bradley says they don't want any trouble or unexpected action from the horses, ranch hands, prowlers, or anything else."

For the second time, Retta noticed Dallas glance toward the main house. At the moment, all the heavy white draperies were drawn against the hot afternoon sun. There was no movement, no one in sight.

"Is there anything wrong, Dallas? Doesn't Mrs. Bradley know I'm here?"

"Nothing wrong," he said quickly. "In fact, she asked me to show you around."

"Good," she said. "I want to see everything, where you work, where you live . . ."

He slipped his hand into one of the rear pockets of her new jeans, pulling her closer to him as they walked.

In the first corral, a half dozen young Arabians stood under a canopy of palm-leaf shade. A pair of colts skittered over to the fence as Dallas leaned on it. He rubbed each between the eyes, then let them lick the palms of his hands. "Arabians like attention," he said. "I spent an hour today making friends with this group."

There was a single horse in the next paddock. At the sound of footsteps, the big mare, a bay with a platinum mane, ambled over to the fence. Retta reached out to smooth the muzzle. It was as soft as velvet to her fingertips, and the horse looked at her trustingly with bright, hazel eyes shaded by lashes as stiff and fair as barnyard straw.

"Isn't she a beauty?" Dallas asked. "She's called Estrella."

"She looks a little fat to me," Retta said.

"That's because she's in foal, Retta. Ordinarily, a breeder wouldn't want a fine mare like this to be pregnant in the hot summer months. Mrs. Bradley explained that the stud they wanted for her was going to be moved to Kentucky."

He ran a hand over Estrella's silken cheek. "This mare is not due to foal till mid-September. I'll be gone by then, but she's in my care for the next three months.

"When her time comes, she'll be brought to that birthing shed." Retta looked toward the square white building at which he was pointing. "I can't show you the inside. It's kept locked and sterile, like any delivery room."

After the corrals, they examined the outdoor lots, the tack rooms, and the storage sheds. The two walked side by side for a quarter of a mile out to the broad back "sand pastures" of the ranch, nearly a hundred acres of natural desert covered with a thin layer of sand that glittered with quartz and mica bits.

Beyond, almost barren of vegetation, the wild,

open desert shimmered off into the distance, then blended with the base of the mountains.

"It's beautiful," Retta said. "But so big, so empty, it's kind of frightening."

"No one's ever built here, no one really lived here. It's just like it always was, like thousands of years ago," Dallas said, staring out at the shimmering horizon.

By the time they had walked back from the pasture, Retta could feel perspiration running down the back of her neck, dampening her T-shirt. She was thirsty and the inside of her nostrils was dry as she breathed.

At one side of the main door, beneath an outdoor faucet, grew a bed of coarse green mint plants. The mint gave off a pungent peppermint scent, a falsely cool aroma in the pulsing temperatures.

"That tap water will be warm," Dallas said. "We'll get something to drink inside as soon as I finish with the horses."

Retta waited patiently while he detached and rubbed down the four exercising horses and led them to an outdoor, frond-covered corral.

As he flung open the big barn door, Retta heard the sound of classical music. "For us?" she asked.

"Mostly for them," Dallas said. "Arabians are sensitive and get bored easily. Music keeps the stables calm."

The barn did seem orderly to Retta. It smelled of hay, wet cement, oil and leather, and the stringent ammonia odor of manure. There were eight horses housed here and Dallas stopped to pet each silken head as it appeared over the half-gating of the individual stalls.

The portable radio hanging from a wooden peg was now playing a waltz. "The Gomez brothers told me Mrs. B. chewed them out one day when they switched to hard rock," Dallas said with a laugh. "She wants things *her* way."

Inside the last stall, looking out with cool gray eyes, was a mare the color of tarnished silver.

"This is Arista," Dallas said. "She's off limits to everyone except the Bradleys and me. I gave them a demonstration today and I have permission to ride her."

He swung open the stall door and grasped Arista by the halter. "Isn't she a beauty?"

Retta smiled. "Yes, and she seems to know it."

"Arista is the pride of this ranch," Dallas said with admiration. "Her bloodlines reach back practically to the pharaohs. On top of that, she's a trained trick horse, five years in a top Polish circus. Poles are great horse trainers, Mrs. Bradley told me. This mare is worth hundreds of thousands of dollars. I can't even guess how much."

The big horse tried to nuzzle the young man's hand. "I'll bring you a sugar cube next time, lady," he said, shutting the stall door.

"Dallas, I'm so thirsty," Retta said, "Can we get something to drink at your bunkhouse?"

"One last place to show you," he said, patting the key ring on his belt. At the far end of the barn, he opened the double lock on a door of solid wood, painted red except for a small window covered with mesh wiring.

Inside was a large room, lit by ceiling lamps and cooled by a window air-conditioner. In it were a desk, several chairs, and filing cabinets. One wall was decorated with horse photographs and a colorful array of award ribbons. A special area had been equipped as a veterinarian's workshop with double stainless-steel sinks, a refrigerator, and cabinets of syringes and medical tools. A third wall was shelved completely with medical books and journals.

"Seems to be a bit of everything here," Retta commented.

Dallas nodded. "Mrs. Bradley and an accountant go over the books here twice a month. I'll work on the daily records and expenses. The refrigerator is mostly for perishable medicines. I can give oral dosages, even some of the cold shots, but for any serious illness or accident, I call Dr. Meacham. All emergency numbers are here and next to the phone in my place. I'll be alone on the ranch nights when the Bradleys stay in Scottsdale."

"And all those books?" Retta asked.

"A library on horses, horse care, horse medicine, horse breeding — horse everything," Dallas said. "Mrs. Bradley says I can read out here or take anything back to my room."

He opened the refrigerator. "This was the boss's idea. I stocked up on soft drinks out here," he said. "What kind do you want?"

Retta looked at the metal shelves holding labeled boxes and bottles, several corked vials of liquid, and soft drinks in cans. "How about straight ginger ale?" Dallas asked. "That should help your thirst." He took out a frosted can.

She walked to the other side of the room. "You've

got to excuse me, Dallas, but I couldn't drink that. It just doesn't seem right to keep human drinks in there with all that horse medicine and urine samples, or whatever that is."

He put the ginger ale back and closed the refrigerator door. "Now that you put it that way, Retta, I'm not thirsty, either."

To change the subject, Retta pointed to the fourth wall of the room. There was a second red door there, with several reinforcing metal bars and a triple lock.

"Where does that strange door lead?" she asked.

"It doesn't *go* anywhere," he said. "It's a walk-in vault."

"A *vault?*" she said, genuinely curious. "Is it for the records on Arabian bloodlines or what?"

"No, those pedigree papers are kept in that locked file, over by the desk," he said. "This is a storage vault, kind of a tack room for valuables. The Bradleys go in for fancy gear — expensive, handmade stuff. A lot of big-time horse people do.

"Mrs. Bradley showed me the Rancho Arabian collection this morning. Some of the things they own, saddles and bridles and hoof trims, they bought in Morocco. One bridle and headband was made in Mexico nearly a hundred years ago . . . leather, turquoise, and pure silver."

"Do you have a key to the vault?"

He touched the key ring on his belt. "Each lock is different. I have three keys. The Brandleys have duplicates and so does their lawyer. No one else. Not even the Gomez brothers."

"Open it, will you?" she asked. "I'd love to see that silver-and-turquoise bridle."

Dallas stepped to the red door, then hesitated.

51

"Mrs. Bradley was specific. Open only in case of fire or earthquake, something like that. I don't think she'd *want* me to let you inside."

"Really, Dallas," Retta said with annoyance. "Lighten up. I won't touch their precious things. I just want to *look*."

He slid both hands deep into his jeans pocket. "I'd like to, Retta, but I just can't. She was definite about it. It's one of the rules."

"You mean those rules she mentioned this morning? What else is there? I don't want to make mistakes over things I don't even know about." Retta waited for his answer.

"Well, the basic rules are pretty much what you'd expect for a place like this," Dallas said. "First and foremost, regular and prompt care and feeding of the stock at all times.

"There's a hot plate in my room for soup or morning coffee. I take the rest of my meals with the family in the main house. If the Bradleys are out of town, I make my own food.

"No loud rock music at any time, no loud TV or radio in my quarters or in this lab-library room after ten at night. No leaving the ranch unattended without permission. No personal calls during working hours. Keep a record of any long distance calls I make and remit tab monthly. Payday is every Thursday, local bank stays open till eight on Friday night."

"It all sounds reasonable," Retta said.

"I'm not finished yet. There's more."

"All right. I'm listening."

He began to tick off the next set of rules on his fingers as he spoke. "No hard liquor for the ranch hands. No pot smoking. No smoking in feed lots, barns, anywhere horses may be in or near, including this room."

"Common sense instructions," Retta said, "nothing you probably wouldn't decide for yourself. And you don't smoke anyway. Is that all?"

"Just about," he said.

"Then let's go." She moved toward the door. "I want to see where you're going to stay. Maybe I can help you unpack. We can plan what extra snacks to buy for the hot plate and — "

He said nothing for a moment, but his face turned serious. "You're not going to like this, Retta," he said, "but there's one major rule I didn't tell you about." He hesitated. "The rule is about visitors. Mrs. Bradley wants no females in my quarters at any time. Not to chat, not to listen to the radio, not even to use the facilities. No one. Not ever."

Retta felt her cheeks get hot with resentment. "No *females* . . . who was Mrs. Bradley expecting you to have?"

"She was polite about it," Dallas said insistently. "In fact, it's an old western tradition, no ladies in the bunkhouse. Any cowboy can tell you that."

He chose his next words carefully. "She specifically doesn't want me to entertain you in my quarters. She doesn't want you to spend the night here."

For a moment, Retta was so stunned she could not put her anger into words. "But I never planned to spend the night, not tonight, or any night! None of this came up when I asked them to hire you. In fact, they *urged* me to help with the nighttime chores. You're going to have to be here nearly every evening, Dallas. Where do the Bradleys expect us to *be?*"

"We can use this lab room anytime. Mrs. Bradley made that clear. It's cool, there's a radio — and a lot of books I want to read."

In her chagrin, Retta was persistent. "Is it because she has a fourteen-year-old son who might be curious about us? Doesn't she know I have a wonderful brother that age myself?"

Dallas shrugged. "I'm a hired hand, I take orders. Try to understand, Retta."

"They seemed so impressed a couple of weeks ago when I said how dependable you are," Retta said.

"This is about big money, Retta. I'm nineteen years old; Mrs. Bradley pointed that out. With the other stock, the equipment, Arista, and Estrella with the foal she's carrying, they're giving me the responsibility of half a million dollars or more. The boss wants me to focus on my work, concentrate on the Arabians, and keep my eyes on the TV monitor when necessary."

"I'd like to talk with Mrs. Bradley," Retta said. "This is so unfair. *I'm* not her hired hand. . . ."

"I don't want you talking with her," Dallas said sharply. "Maybe you're not a hired hand, but you're the hired hand's girlfriend right now."

"Oh, I'm sorry," Retta said contritely. "I shouldn't have said what I just said." She reached out to touch his bare arm. "Dallas, you said you could take time off tonight. I just don't like Rancho Arabian much right now. . . ."

He took her hand. "Let's go then. Eddie Gomez told me about a place."

Following his directions, Henrietta drove the yellow car over back roads to the Bunking Bronco

54

Tavern. Even though the evening was still bright, the outdoor sign had been turned on — a neon picture of a horse curled up on a bunk bed, a striped nightcap on his head. A couple of dusty pickup trucks stood side by side in the gravel lot.

The small tavern was empty except for a man at the cash register and two customers drinking beer at the end of the bar. Much of the light in the dim room came from an illuminated cigarette machine and a TV set over the bar. A baseball game was in progress with the sound turned off.

As Retta and Dallas slipped into a booth along the wall, the man at the cash register put a Willie Nelson tape into a deck and walked toward them.

"What'll you have?" he asked.

"I'd like soup and a salad," Retta said.

The man shook his head. "We got chips, peanuts, and pretzels. And for a sandwich, barbecued beef. That's all."

"Good enough," Dallas said with a look at Retta. "Make that three barbecues and two colas. Unless you want a second sandwich, too?" Retta shook her head.

They sat waiting in silence, fingers touching on the scarred tabletop. From the far end of the room came the rhythmic hum of an old-fashioned air conditioner set into the wall. Water dripped steadily from the cooling unit into two buckets of sand, making soft, wet sounds. The western music provided a muted background, blending together the other rhythms in the dim, moist room.

Later, as Dallas ate his second sandwich, Retta watched him across the table. The backs of his hands were already reddened by the desert sun and a new color burned on his cheekbones, making his eyes a cool gray-green.

When he finished eating, she reached across the table to slip the knotted kerchief from his forehead. The sunburned skin felt almost feverish to her touch.

"You're already changing color," she said.

She folded her hand around the soda glass, cold with ice cubes, but the warmth, the smooth touch of his skin, did not leave her fingertips.

"You seem so far away," she said tentatively. "You might as well still be in Philadelphia."

Dallas Dobson slid out of his side of the booth and moved in beside her, stretching his long legs under the table and sliding down on the bench until they were sitting close and evenly, shoulder to shoulder. "Now I'm not in Philadelphia," he said.

"If you're tired we don't even have to talk," Retta suggested.

He closed his eyes for a moment. "I *am* tired, but I want to listen."

Speaking softly, she told him something about her day, the meeting with her father, the agreement to write two stories a week.

He squeezed her hand. "I'm proud of you, Retta. I didn't know you could write things like that."

"Neither did I," she said. "I'm not good at it yet. I was in the mall two hours and it took me another two hours to write the story. I think I redid it six times."

"Do I have to wait till the paper comes out to read what you wrote?" Dallas asked.

"No. I brought you a copy but felt sort of shy about it. It's in the car."

"Good. I'll read it tonight, back at the ranch." He

looked thoughtful. "Let me ask you something, Retta. Two hours in the mall, then two hours at the office — does that mean you were out of your house most of the day?"

"I was home in the morning for a while and then before I came back to meet you. Why?"

"Did you or your family get a call from my father?"

"No," she said with surprise. "Why?"

"I thought he might have tried to reach me."

"Wouldn't he have tried to reach you at the ranch?"

"I was working out in the corrals a good part of the afternoon," he said obliquely.

"Why would he call? You just got here," Retta said.

"I thought that's what families did when someone took a trip — call to see if that person got there safely."

"Sometimes. Not always," Retta said gently.

"He *planned* to drive me to the airport," Dallas went on, "but something came up. I suppose he had a few drinks over it."

"That 'something' that came up," Retta said, "was it about us, or maybe just about me?"

Dallas seemed startled. "What makes you think that?"

"Charlotte Amberson. She called me this morning. Charlie told me Junior Provanza told her that you and your father had a big argument before you left. From the way she talked, I think that argument was about you and me. Am I right?"

Dallas nodded. "I'll tell you if you want me to," he said. "But remember, you asked, okay?"

She put her hand on his.

"My old man didn't want me to come out here this summer. He didn't say so outright, but he made it seem as if I was deserting him. He acted like I was choosing between him and you." Dallas shrugged. "Even when I'm home he doesn't spend much time there. He just wants to know I'm around."

"You can't blame him for that," Retta said.

"He should have let me go," Dallas said. "He knew how much it meant to me. The afternoon before I left, we argued, really hot. He said something I couldn't take. He said he thought three thousand miles was a long way to go to kiss a girl. I couldn't let him talk about you that way. He shouldn't have said what he did."

"That's *all?*" Retta said in surprise. "There's nothing wrong with that, not really. You're too sensitive, Dallas."

Dallas stood up and counted out several dollars onto the tabletop. "My father was more blunt," he said quietly. "That isn't exactly what he said."

He looked away, so she could not read his eyes. Impulsively, Retta pulled the car keys from her pocket and tossed them on the table. "Here, Dallas," she said. "You drive."

Later, as they approached the big tamarisk hedge, Dallas slowed the car, but Retta put a hand on the steering wheel and said, "It's late. You have to be up at five and I've got a new job, remember? . . ."

So much had happened for both of them during this emotional day. First, the strange reunion, the unexpected challenge of the newspaper job, then the disturbing rule from Mrs. Bradley, and now the rumbling, distant trouble with the older Dobson.

58

Retta could not help the small sigh that escaped her.

"What does that mean?" Dallas asked.

"Nothing much," she said. "It's just your ordinary, summer-in-California type of sigh."

He put an arm around her shoulder. "It was a mistake to tell you about that argument, even if you asked. Forget it, will you, Retta? This is going to be *our* summer, isn't it?"

"Is it?" she asked.

Chapter
5

Even before Dallas flew west, Henrietta had de-cided not to keep a diary, not to have a calendar in her room, not to count the days. She wanted to "be" without thinking why or for how long.

Chores and the needs of the horses quickly developed the pattern for activity at Rancho Arabian. Several times in the first ten days, Retta set her clock early and drove out in the cool of the early morning, the sky barely pink with sunrise, to share a thermos of coffee with Dallas. He was always up, showered and dressed for the day in clean work clothes.

On these mornings, the first twitter of birds, the sound of horses pawing and nickering in the barn and corrals, and the breeze from the mountains, scented bitter with creosote and wild thyme, created a special mesmerizing beauty.

After the wooded fields and narrow, tree-lined roads of rural Pennsylvania, this vast stretch of desert in California seemed to be another world. The flat plateau, with a far horizon of stark mountains, had an atmosphere so clean and stimulating that for Retta there was a new sensation, a feeling that some unseen, powerful source in the center of the planet was pushing Rancho Arabian higher and closer into the sky.

It was a beauty that asked for silence. On those brilliant desert mornings, when Retta helped Dallas with the lighter chores, they found they could be together, close, caring, without speaking or touching.

After breakfast at Desert Lily Street each day, Retta and her brother made beds and put the Caldwell house in order so that Mrs. Caldwell could leave early for the newspaper office. It was light, undemanding work. There was nothing in the new, modern house to soak, scrub, scrape, or polish. Even the desert sands, which sometimes blew in dust clouds along the streets, did not sift through the sealed, plate-glass doors and windows.

At her mother's suggestion, Retta gathered together back issues of the *Palms Gazette* and spent several hours in the newsroom each morning studying the styles and formats of different articles.

After she felt confident enough to try, she managed a good question-and-answer interview with the principal of the new high school. Then her father okayed a short, humorous piece she wrote called,

"A Day in the Life of a Roadrunner." Twice she covered Chamber of Commerce meetings at City Hall to make notes for the paper's regular "City Business" column. With her third paycheck, she bought a small tape recorder to make interviews easier and more accurate.

Most evenings after dinner, Retta changed into jeans and a T-shirt to drive to the ranch and help with evening chores. Several times, Dallas saddled Arista, and Retta watched as he put the mare through her paces.

The trained horse was so highly strung and accustomed to public acclaim that she needed this extra exercise and attention, Dallas told Retta.

"I just have to touch the reins in a certain way and she begins to do her tricks," Dallas said. "I never worked much with a trick horse before, but Sam Houston was good at it."

The Gomez brothers quit work at five o'clock to drive home to Indio, but one evening they stayed late to meet Retta. She and Dallas walked to the area behind the barn where the brothers were hosing down the dusty earth to get ready for the tractor-trailers scheduled to deliver a feed load in the morning.

Both Gomezes were in their late twenties, with stocky, muscular bodies, dark hair, and strong, white teeth.

They were friendly but shy. Each shook Retta's hand and greeted her with a few soft Spanish words. They smiled, then patted Dallas on the back when Retta was able to answer them with a sentence or two in their own language.

Later, when the brothers roared out the front gate

in their pickup truck, Dallas touched Retta lightly on the cheek. "You're nice," he said. "They'd been kidding me. By my age, they were both married and had babies. Big, *macho* stuff. So I wanted to show you off."

By the end of the third week, Retta felt confident enough to take on the evening ritual of bathing down Estrella. Dallas showed her how to lead the pregnant mare into the grooming area, back the animal carefully between two metal hold-bars, and fasten the lead rope to a stanchion.

She used buckets of water, sudsy with horse shampoo, and a natural sponge to soak down the great swollen body from forelock to hock, letting the warm liquid clean off the sweat and dust of the day and sluice over the tired muscles stretched with the burden of pregnancy.

The horse seemed grateful, standing patient, trusting, watching Retta's movements with her great eyes, never stirring except for a twitch of the tail or an occasional involuntary spasm as the unborn colt moved suddenly inside, sending a ripple reaction over the taut barrel of her body.

"I don't know much about horses," Retta said one evening as Dallas was helping her rinse and towel down, "but Estrella seems very pregnant to me. I mean, *very pregnant*."

"Don't worry," he said. "I told you, she's not due till September. The Bradleys won't be in Scottsdale then, you can be sure. This foal is going to be an event." He rubbed his hand soothingly over the diamond-shaped star, silver-white, directly between Estrella's dark eyes.

"Look at those markings," Retta said. "It's as if someone used an eyeliner around her eyes."

"Those distinctive markings are a trait of good Arabians," Dallas said. "And did you know that Arabian horses have the largest eyes in the animal world except for whales?"

"No, I didn't," Retta said, "and I don't remember you knowing all that much about Arabians back in Pennsylvania, either," she said, smiling.

He laughed. "I didn't. I've been taking horse books from the library back to the bunkhouse at night."

As Dallas began to collect the wet towels, Retta reached up and, with her fingers, combed out the short tuft of hair between the mare's eyes.

"Dallas," she said. "I'd like you to know more about what *I* do. My parents want you for dinner the next night you're free. I'll take you over to the newspaper first."

"I'd like that," he said. "I can be off Friday."

While he led Estrella back to her stall, Retta leaned against the corral railing, looking out over the stillness of the desert night. Except for a little breeze in the palms, the only sound she heard was Dallas's voice, talking to the pregnant horse, a lulling singsong of affection and reassurance.

Even though Dallas asked questions, the tour of the *Palms Gazette* offices took less than a half hour.

"Of course, the press equipment is all shut down this time of day," Retta explained, almost apologetically, as she lowered the air-conditioning and snapped off the lights in the main office. "Everything is more interesting when people are at work."

"I'd watch if you want to show me how you write something," Dallas offered.

Retta laughed. "Come on," she said. "Poppy told me he'd put the steaks on the grill promptly at a quarter to seven. I've already showed you everything I know."

After dinner it was Mrs. Caldwell who suggested iced coffee on the terrace. Darkness had just begun to shade the garden and a pale half-moon laid its flat white image on the surface of the pool. For a moment, there was no sound except the movement of glassware on the tabletop and the tinkle of ice cubes.

Connie Caldwell said unexpectedly, "I don't know why I think about the past and what used to be, when everything is so exciting and new in California." For a moment her voice was touched with sadness. "At this time of day — dusk, I mean — my mind turns back to Pennsylvania. Everyone at this table, except Dallas, of course, was born right there in Zenith County."

"No reason to forget that beautiful countryside," her husband said gently. "Nor the fact that before the highway, we had the life we wanted."

"Maybe I'm still a small-town girl," his wife said. "I guess I expected to spend all my life there."

In the thin moonlight, Retta could not quite make out the expression in Dallas's eyes, but she knew by the way he cleared his throat, then shifted his chair at the end of the table, that he had something to say but had not decided how to say it.

Finally, he spoke out. "I drove by your farm many times after you left, Mrs. Caldwell. In fact, last week

I stopped at the gate and looked up the drive."

"I don't think I'd have the courage to do that right now," she said.

"Everything looked good," he assured her, "almost as if you still lived there. The whole north side of the farm pond, where the highway bulldozed down your woods, that's graded now. The area is planted with fir trees, pretty big ones, no more than three feet apart. Someone is looking to grow quick cover to block out the highway."

"Fir trees . . ." Retta's mother said.

"Of course the meadow is green this time of year," Dallas went on hurriedly. "It had been mowed recently. I could still smell the hay. The blossoms were gone in the apple orchard but the lilac hedges, the big ones that Retta told me you planted yourself the year you got married, they were still in bloom the day I stopped by. We had a cold, wet spring," he said. "Lilacs love that weather."

The people on the terrace were silent then, each wandering in his or her own train of thought. A light wind had sprung up, rustling the palm fronds and sending a riffle across the face of the pond. The yellow jasmine vines climbing the rear wall of the garden were honey-scented, giving out an aroma that was heady and sticky-sweet in the warmth of the evening.

When Dallas spoke again, his thoughts were still at the farm in Pennsylvania. "That's probably the prettiest lilac hedge in our county, Mrs. Caldwell. I'd never seen pink lilacs before. I told my father about them."

"They're Persian lilacs," Mrs. Caldwell said. "I bought them at an old plant nursery that used to be out near the Provanzas' store. It was a sentimental choice. I had just found out I was pregnant. I thought the flower clusters looked like pink lace and I secretly hoped for a little girl. A girl first, then a boy, just as they came."

"The scent from those flowers came right out to the gate," Dallas said.

"I planted that hedge nearly eighteen years ago," Connie Caldwell went on. "This is the first spring I haven't seen it in bloom."

She reached over to pat Dallas's big, sunburned hand as it lay on the table. "You were thoughtful to check out that way. Thank you, Dallas."

Later, when they are alone in the kitchen, putting things in the dishwasher, Retta said, "I'm glad you told Mother about the lilacs. But you must have seen other things at our place."

"Some," he said. "The highway department plans to open all six lanes by September first, so there's been a lot of paving going on. There are still trucks and heavy equipment all over the property.

"And the motel people who bought your house want to have the remodeling completed so they can open the same day as the highway. There's lumber and plasterboard piled up under tarps on the front lawn. The last day I looked in, the workmen were just beginning to break out the back wall to make your kitchen bigger. There's a sign posted out front: 'Red Fox Inn. Opening September 1.' "

He took a pair of rinsed plates from Retta and placed them in the dishwasher. "They cut down those two old buttonwood trees, Retta," he said. "The ones you told me you could see from your bedroom."

She felt a deep stab of pain and loss, as if she could see and almost hear the blue-sky emptiness where those great trees had stood.

"They had to do it," Dallas said. "That's where the new parking lot will be."

"I'm so glad you didn't tell Mother that. She put feed out under those buttonwoods, especially in the snow. Pheasants nested there. I think she worried more about the wild things than about Two and me."

"Would they ever go back to Pennsylvania, your parents, I mean?"

"No." Retta shook her head emphatically. "To visit, maybe, but to live — never. Losing that land, selling the house — it all hurt too much. They're beginning to heal, I think."

Dallas closed the dishwasher and wiped off the kitchen counter with a paper towel. He stood behind Retta for a moment, then put his arms around her and drew her tight against him, so that the top of his chin rested on her hair. She could feel the soft rise and fall of his breathing.

"I can't go back, either, Dallas," she said softly, leaning against him. "The Caldwell family just doesn't live there anymore. I *have* thought about it. So it must have crossed your mind."

"Every day," he said. "And whenever I think about September."

On three separate evenings in one week, Henrietta dialed the Amberson number in Pennsylvania. Each time she waited through eight rings, imagining the interior of the old brick house she knew so well echoing over and over with the shrill bell tones. Either no one was home, she decided, or no one was at home who wanted to answer the phone.

One night, sitting with Dallas as he leafed through a horse manual in the lab-library, Retta wrote a four-page letter to Charlie.

"No matter what I tell her, she'll be disappointed," Retta said as she slipped the letter into a stamped envelope. "Charlie's like her mother. They always want gossip or some inside story instead of getting into real life themselves."

"Life can't be much fun for her. You're gone, she's stuck out in the country," he said.

"That's why I worry about her," Retta said contritely. "I'll try to write more often. In fact, I'll drop this letter off at the post office tonight."

"Good idea," Dallas said, turning a page. "Mail does seem slow between here and Pennsylvania. I wrote one letter and three postcards already and I still haven't heard from my father."

A week later, after driving back from the ranch, Retta found an envelope from Charlotte Amberson waiting for her on the hall table. Determined to set her alarm clock early, she left the letter unopened for the next day.

In the morning, shortly after five-thirty, she parked her car outside the Bradleys' gate and walked in quietly, moving up the long gravel drive in her light sandals. Dallas opened the door to his quarters at the first knock, putting a finger to his lips. They crossed the yard, went through the long, dim barn where the Arabians were just stirring from sleep, and exited into the feed lot at the rear of the stable.

She handed him a thermos. "Fresh coffee," she said in a soft voice. "I made it not half an hour ago."

"Great," he said. "I like yours better than the instant brew I make on the hot plate." He poured steaming coffee into two plastic thermos cups, handed her one, then settled himself on the sandy ground, leaning back on a square bale of dried alfalfa. "And, Retta, we don't have to whisper back here. We're the only ones awake."

Retta selected a second bundle of sweet-smelling hay and settled back against it. "A letter from Charlotte came yesterday," she said. "I saved it to read to you."

Dallas balanced the coffee cup on the rough ground, then lay back contentedly, both hands behind his head. "Tell me about Charlotte," he said.

She took the envelope from her pocket and tore it open. The lines were typed, but some of the letters were blurred and Retta knew her friend was using the old typewriter, the one Carter Caldwell had given Charlie's mother years before to write the society column for their Zenith paper.

Retta read aloud: " *'Dear Sphinx: Your letter came today and I just reread same. Though you obviously don't want me as your confidante, I can read between the lines.*

" *'What I mean to say is that letter tells me your personal life right now is hot enough to combust. Well, I'm glad for you. Remember, you're having fun for two these days, because your best friend isn't having* any.' "

Charlotte went on for several paragraphs about the humid summer weather, the fact that her mother rarely answered the phone anymore because she dreaded bill collectors, and that chasing a muskrat out of the cellar was the most excitement that she —

Charlie, Jr. — had enjoyed since school let out.

" *'And now the real news. My mother worked four days at Mullins Pharmacy (your father called Mr. Mullins and asked for the favor) and I thought our financial troubles were over, but she quit. She says she resigned rather than sell cigarettes to old Mrs. Curtayne. But Mrs. Curtayne has had that cough for years. It's kind of her trademark, right?*

" *'I think Mother was fired. She was late for work all four days and she just isn't a good salesperson. You know how sharp-tongued she gets when she's nipping the Madeira.*

" *'Now she insists she'll work full-time on the novel. Sometimes she goes out at night to bars and discos to "observe life" for her book. And she does look rather sweet in jeans and that cowboy jacket.*

" *'Sudden thought:* Could my mother be seeing someone? *No, let's forget that crazy idea.*

" *'Besides not figuring how to keep us in food money, Mater has gone loony in the age department. Now she says I can't go out with Junior because I'm too young. At the movies the other night (I broke open my piggy bank), she tried to tell the cashier I was* twelve. *Me, who's almost into a C cup and couldn't pass for twelve if I walked on my knees.' "*

"I didn't know she was suddenly going to talk about bust measurements," Retta said.

"We all know Charlotte's a big girl," Dallas said. "What else does she write?"

Retta glanced down at the letter. "Nothing, really. She's reading a book about Eskimos, there's the makings of minestrone soup growing in the garden she planted, and she wishes her mother hadn't sold her bicycle.

"She adds a P.S. *'Give that big hunk, Dallas, a kiss for me and, while you're at it, have one yourself.'*"

Dallas moved his coffee cup, rolled over on one elbow, and reached out toward Retta. "Come on over here," he said. "Charlie's orders."

At that moment, they both became aware for the first time of the sound of a human voice and the hard tap of boots on the cement floor in the barn. Someone was in there, moving from stall to stall, murmuring to the Arabians. The voice tones were casual, the pace of the footsteps slow, deliberately unhurried. Then they stopped.

There was a pause, a long, listening silence before Mrs. Bradley called out, "Dallas? Are you around somewhere? I need you to do something for me."

"Out here in the feed lot," he answered.

Moments later, when Mrs. Bradley stepped through the rear stable door, she shaded her eyes and blinked a little in the morning light. Retta was seated on an alfalfa bale and Dallas was standing nearby, sipping coffee.

"Do you need something, ma'am?" Dallas asked quietly.

"Yes, if you please. Saddle up Arista for me. I'm going to take her out for a ride before the day turns hot."

Dallas poured the dregs of coffee out on the sandy ground and handed the cup to Retta. "Right away, ma'am," he said and walked into the barn.

Mrs. Bradley was wearing white jeans with a black cotton shirt and short white riding boots. Her fair hair was pulled back, tied with a ribbon. A pair of sunglasses was hooked to the pocket of her blouse. She turned to smile at Retta, but the smile was cool.

"Do you do this often? Bring coffee out in the early morning, I mean?"

"Yes and no," Retta said. "I don't do it every day, but I *have* done it before. I'm sorry I woke you. I parked — "

"Oh, please," Mrs. Bradley interrupted. "Don't apologize. I was already awake." And then, "Are your parents such early risers?"

"No," Retta said. "But they know I sometimes drive out here to see Dallas before he starts work."

Retta stood, screwed both cups back on the thermos, and brushed the straw off the seat of her jeans. "Please tell me, Mrs. Bradley, if it's something you'd rather I didn't do."

Mrs. Bradley put on her sunglasses and her eyes were suddenly dark, opaque circles. "Use your own judgment, my dear," she said. "We have some very, very valuable stock on the ranch this summer. And we put a lot of trust in Dallas. He's working out well and we depend on him. But too often, I've found, lady friends and horses just don't mix."

Retta felt the sharp sting of tears in her eyes. She did not know if they came from anger at the woman's chiding words or from the sudden disappointment that flooded her thoughts. She blinked once, kept her voice calm. "Dallas appreciates your confidence," she said. "He likes working here."

"Yes, I believe he does," Mrs. Bradley said. "And I'm glad you're so understanding about this, Retta."

Back at the car, Henrietta threw the empty thermos into the backseat and slid behind the wheel.

73

Without looking back, she revved up the motor, then sent up clouds of dust as she swung onto the narrow road and past the tamarisk trees toward Thirty-nine Palms.

It was the loss of these morning hours that distressed her. The time seemed so important while the day was still cool and sweet to the senses and their world was small and private.

Before Mrs. Bradley had come to the feed lot, Retta had decided to ask Dallas to spend all of tomorrow, his day off, with her. It would be a significant date for them both, the first day of July, the beginning of the second month of summer.

Almost one third of their important time together was already gone. And Mrs. Bradley had just vetoed their mornings.

He remembered. It was late when he called; every last chore was done and he was back in the bunkhouse for the night.

"I'm off tomorrow, Retta," he said.

"I know."

"All right if I come for you about ten? I'll get the Gomezes started on a couple of things, then I'll take off."

"I'll be ready."

"By the way, Mrs. Bradley stopped by a few minutes ago to bring me the newspaper with your roadrunner article in it. I said you'd showed it to me. She said to tell you she thought it was good."

"Thank you for the message, Dallas," Retta said tartly, "but I don't really care what she thinks."

"Yes, you do, Retta. We both do. You wouldn't be angry if you didn't."

She decided to change the subject. "Did I mention that my father wants me to work on something tomorrow, just the research part? It shouldn't take long. And I'd like to stop at the high school to register."

"We can do all that together," he said. "I've got the whole day, you know. Retta, Mrs. Bradley also mentioned she's glad you've been giving Estrella extra care — the bathing and rubdowns. She says serenity is so important to successful birthing."

"Dallas, do you have to talk so much about Mrs. Bradley?"

"No," he said. "I don't. But I also want you to know that she told me about your conversation. She said you seemed to agree with her that early-morning visitors aren't a good idea. . . ."

"I suppose I agreed. After all, as you say, she's the boss." Retta sighed.

"She *is*," he said succinctly. "Now I've passed on everything Mrs. Bradley told me. Tomorrow we don't even have to mention her name, okay? It's the first of July, you know."

Chapter
6

O ne wing of the new school was double-storied.
The rest of the structure, an angular, modern
building, adobe-finished, with rows of wide windows, sprawled over nearly two acres. The roof was
crowned with a web of air-conditioning ducts,
painted a bright blue. Desert shrubs and Washing-
tonia palms had been planted around the grounds.

The main doors were unlocked and inside the
building there was a smell of new wood. In the office
area, Retta and Dallas found a single teacher working at a desk. A lean, fair-haired man with an easy
smile, he identified himself as Dennis Jory, head of
the English department.

Retta introduced herself and Dallas, then explained that she was new in Thirty-nine Palms and

wanted to register for the fall term. Mr. Jory went to another desk and returned with enrollment forms.

"Fill these out," he said. "Be sure to sign the section that gives us permission to send for your records from the last school."

"That's Havendale High in Zenith, Pennsylvania, Mr. Jory," Dallas said. "Last year we both went there."

"Oh? You've graduated?" the teacher asked.

Dallas shook his head. "No. I need some credits. But I expect to make it by January."

"I see," Mr. Jory said. "Then you'll be with us for *one* semester?"

"No, sir," Dallas said. "I can't do that. I'm expected back home. I came along today because I want to see where my girlfriend will be."

Mr. Jory looked thoughtful, then said, "This is a bit irregular since the building won't be officially open for several weeks, but perhaps you and Miss Caldwell might like to have a personal tour."

He opened a desk drawer, separated two keys from a ring, and handed them to Dallas.

"This opens the entrance to the main classrooms," he said. "And this one is the key to the library on the tower floor. We're proud of the library, though we aren't budgeted for half the books we need.

"I'll be here for another hour or so," Mr. Jory added.

Their footsteps echoed in hollow unison through the halls. "I'm sure I'll get lost the first day," Retta said in a hushed voice.

"It'll all seem different with people in it." Dallas

put his hand on her shoulder. "You'll be all right."

The big classrooms were bright with daylight from tinted windows set near the ceiling to protect against the direct dazzle of the desert sun. Rows of chairs with desk arms, in alternate oranges and blues, were placed on noiseproof tile floors, the color of wind-swept sand.

The chemistry lab was the largest of all the classrooms, walled with glass-doored cabinets and equipped with worktables, complete with stainless-steel sinks, electrical outlets, and Bunsen burners.

Dallas strolled to the rear of the laboratory, selected a table, and leaned on it with his elbows. He looked steadily around the big lab, seeming to be studying every detail. "This is where the teacher would put me, at the back of the room," he said. "Ever since kindergarten, I've been the tallest in my class."

Retta smiled. "I remember. Just like your first day at Havendale High, when Mr. Engel told you to sit behind me."

As they left the lab, a subtle change seemed to touch his mood. Retta was aware as they walked back through the empty halls to the tower building that she no longer felt his hand warm on her shoulder.

The new library filled the entire top floor of the two-storied structure. Here, at this higher elevation, windows at three sides of the room had been installed to frame a different desert scene. One tier showed a group of distant palms that seemed to be etched on the shimmering air. Another caught a dramatic stretch of wild, wax-leafed creosote bushes, and the third row framed a panorama of the purple-hued Santa Rosa mountains far beyond Thirty-nine Palms.

Retta was awed by the unexpected beauty and turned to catch Dallas's reaction, but he was staring out silently at the landscape, his thoughts obviously somewhere else.

At the exit door of the classroom building, he stopped. "I'd like to look at that chemistry lab again," he said.

She walked back with him and waited just outside the door. He strolled to the rear of the room, pulled a high stool up to a worktable, folded his hands, and looked toward the front blackboard, as if waiting for a teacher to call class to order.

After a moment, he turned on a water spigot so a slim, silver stream ran into the sink, switched the Bunsen burner on and off to see if it was connected, then opened the three equipment drawers under the worktable.

Retta had never seen him like this, so absorbed in himself, almost playacting, trying to pretend to be a new student in chemistry class. It was credits in Senior Chemistry, she knew, which he hoped to earn by January, back at Havendale High.

"All right, that's that, Retta," he called out suddenly, as if she too had made some decision. "If we're going to drive to the church for your newspaper, we'd better start. I'll bring the truck around from the parking lot. You take the keys back to the office."

"Get me about six hundred words on St. Francis of the Rocks for Saturday's paper," Carter Caldwell had told his daughter. "It's an architectural gem, but a ready-made anachronism. That Italian director, Fiero Ferme, donated all the money. Kind of a thank-you for his success in Hollywood. We've got a medieval church right in the middle of a twentieth century desert."

Retta was unprepared for the surprising beauty of the church itself, white-walled and red-roofed, peaked with double bell towers and standing on a stretch of mountain-backed desert a few miles out of Thirty-nine Palms. Dallas turned the pickup truck into a curved drive, then proceeded to a parking spot.

St. Francis had been built to face miles of open country, but the rear entrance was backed almost into the mountains. Behind and above it, a single mountain towered in jagged rises, three times the height of the bell towers, with a giant spill of brown volcanic rock that clung to the steep slopes like solid lava.

Inside the church, the great, hanging iron chandeliers were unlit, the high, vaulted ceilings touched with shadows.

There was no air-conditioning, yet the interior of the church was cool with the coolness of thick stone, and smelled both scented and damp from wisps of incense left from morning mass and from holy water puddled in marble fonts inside the entry doors.

"Wait for me," Reta whispered. "I'll just walk around and make some notes." Dallas nodded and went down an aisle toward the back of the church, his cowboy boots making a staccato rhythm on the tile. Above him, at the rear of the building, was an ornate choir loft, centered by a round stained glass window filled with heavenly blossoms, flying angels, and kneeling saints.

Dallas paused to look back at Retta at the very moment he stepped into the illuminated spot the great choir window cast on the church floor. For a moment, as she looked at him, he was trapped magically in a red, green, yellow, and blue lariat of colored light.

In the intense silence of the church, broken only by the faint guttering of candles, this moment of beauty was so unexpected that Retta was not prepared for the sudden, rapid upbeat of her heart. She could find no thoughts to match her intense emotional reaction to the Dallas Dobson she saw there, tall, handsome, and yet remote, as multicolored and glorious as some distant saint.

As Dallas settled in a pew, she wandered through the church, making notes. Unexpectedly, a priest came out of a door beside the altar and spent a few moments rearranging the mass books and trimming the wicks of votive candles. Then he disappeared again, his long white habit fluttering with the speed of his movements, bright blue Adidas tennis shoes showing beneath the hemline. Retta smiled to herself as she wrote, "Heavenly glimpse — sky-blue shoes."

She walked to a shadowed corner of the church with a full view of the interior and stood there quietly. At this moment, St. Francis of the Rocks seemed to her a minor miracle, a blessed place, serene and ancient, as if it had been part of the desert for at least a century.

Then why, Retta asked herself, in the midst of this beauty, with everything so peaceful, so perfect, why am I so sad? Why do I keep thinking about September, instead of feeling glad for this single, precious afternoon?

As she glanced toward the back of the church, Dallas raised his hand to beckon her. At the pew, he pulled in his long legs and she stepped over them.

Retta folded the notes into her shoulder bag, then settled quietly in the pew, inhaling deeply the faint, smoky spice of incense and watching the hypnotic flicker of the altar candles. Except for the candles and the spreads of colored light from stained glass windows, the church seemed to be filled with an early dusk.

She was aware of Dallas's presence beside her, the bulk of his shoulder, the warmth of his thigh against hers, and the even, measured cadence of his breathing. His angular body was cramped in the narrow pew and he sat with his knees jackknifed high, just as he had so often sat in the yellow car back in Pennsylvania.

He lifted her left hand from her lap and placed it on his knee, spreading the fingers wide on the denim of his jeans. Without speaking, he moved that hand first to the right, then to the left, paused, then repeated the process. Watching him, puzzled, she saw at last what he was trying to do.

From a stained glass window above, a patterned picture shone down around them in a mosaic of shapes and brilliant colors. In that window, a cherubic angel, floating high, was ringed with a small yellow halo, and Dallas continued to move Henrietta's hand gently until the halo reflected exactly on the fourth finger of that hand, a small, ethereal band of gold, a perfect wedding ring.

Retta felt a sharp intake of her own breath and tried, for reasons she did not at that moment understand, to pull her hand away from the small, imprisoning band of light.

His fingers stayed tight and firm on her wrist, holding the hand in place, and when she looked at him, his face was so still and serious that she stopped struggling and put her face against his shoulder.

"We can't, Dallas," she said in a helpless whisper. "We can't get married. We're too young. My parents would never understand. . . ."

She made no attempt to stop the tears, just shut her eyes and felt them warm on her cheeks. Dallas put an arm around her shoulder but released her left hand, now a small clenched fist. He leaned toward her and whispered, without reproach, "You're wrong about that, Retta. *I'm* not too young. You know that."

She looked up at him, wanting to speak, but her mind was a jumble of contrary words and impressions. It was less a moment of joy than one of pounding confusion.

No one warned me it would be Dallas Dobson, she thought wildly. It just happened. That first day I saw him back in Pennsylvania, when I saw his face, I began to like the boy.

I wanted him with me this summer, I needed him, but I still need myself. There is so much I have to do. I'm only the start of a real person. I have to be more.

This was meant to be an interlude, just a three-month summer. I expected to love him, but without decisions. I can't be more than I am, not even for him. I can't be older or wiser. I'm not ready to be another person.

She was aware of Dallas beside her, tense and silent, waiting for her words.

Dear God, she thought, don't let this be some terrible game. I swear, on the beauty of this church, I want to love him. But I can't decide my whole life in one afternoon.

She put her head against his shoulder. "I can't respond to what you just said," she whispered to him, "because no matter what you want, we're on different timetables. For me, what's happening is too soon. I'm asking you . . . please. Whatever you're thinking, it's not right for me yet, Dallas. I need more time."

They sat silent and close for a long time, until the sun outside had begun to descend toward the west and the colors from the big windows above them shifted patterns. The angel's halo, now a brighter, sunburned gold, showed on the back of a pew several rows ahead, and Retta's left hand, no longer tight and closed, rested in shadows.

Finally, without speaking, Dallas nodded to her and they moved from the pew and down the aisle. As they stepped together from the church, the carillon bells in the tall, white *campanellas* began to toll for late afternoon services. A sweep of birds left the towers and rose to circle the church in a flock. The afternoon air was still a brilliant blue-white, and shards of light flashed back from crystal fragments in the mountain rocks.

Retta paused to look up at the ringing bells, then put on her sunglasses before turning to Dallas. But he was watching the strange flight of birds, his face tilted up and away from her, and there was no way she could read whatever thoughts might be behind his eyes.

Chapter
7

There was something almost liquid in the way the long hot days of July began to slip away. Unexpectedly, the last week of the month, the Bradleys decided to fly to Scottsdale by themselves. They left young Burton Bradley at Rancho Arabian with Dallas. The boy studied alone in the main house most of the day, ate a sandwich for lunch, then shared whatever Dallas cooked in the evening.

Each day as the sun began to fade, Burton joined in the final chores — feeding and watering, then cleaning up and walking horses that still needed exercise. He seemed to enjoy working by himself, oiling harnesses or raking up the skittering oleander blossoms that had fallen in the heat of the day.

Burton's help gave Retta more time each evening

for Estrella's therapeutic cleanup. It was a task she now looked forward to. Often, as she moved the soapy sponge over the mare's body, her cheek would press against the animal's great swollen belly. She sometimes felt she could hear the faint heartbeat of the foal growing inside, and her own pulse quickened at the nearness of the eternal miracle.

For seven nights in a row, Retta, Dallas, and Burton Bradley spent several hours together in the cool comfort of the lab-library. Young Bradley brought over a checkerboard from his room and, with the barn radio sounding in the background, he and Retta played the game while Dallas read a book from the stocked shelves.

The room always smelled lightly of wintergreen and rubbing alcohol and the pleasant odor of nearby horses. Burton was a serious checkers player, intent on winning, and Dallas seemed to have forgotten both of them, concentrating, frowning sometimes, as he turned page after page without speaking a word. Even though there was little conversation and no chance at all to be alone, Retta knew that these seven peaceful, oddly intimate evenings, when the three of them seemed almost a family, would stay forever in her memory.

Dallas walked her out to the car each night, kissed her lightly, and touched her cheek with the back of his hand, as if she were a small child. She longed to talk to him about the deeply emotional time together back at the church, but she felt shy, unable to trust herself to find the right words; since that afternoon, he had seemed preoccupied, even remote.

On the final night of the week, he tapped on the window of the car just as she was about to pull away. She rolled it down and he leaned forward on his folded arms, his face just inches from hers. It was a hot, still night and he pulled a red handkerchief from his jeans and dried his face. Then he folded back a corner and wiped away the light sweat that beaded her forehead.

"Don't think I haven't been thinking about us, Retta," he said. "I have. I just haven't said anything about the other day because right now there seems to be nothing to say."

"What do you mean?" she asked.

"A feeling," he said. "Sometimes I'm not sure of you."

Retta felt a touch of panic, a small threatening sense of loss. "You're worrying me," she said. "It's like you're giving me some sort of secret test and I'm not making it."

"It's not just you," he said. "It's something I have to think about. I've got to figure this one out for myself."

Alone in her room that night, Retta was glad to have the new letter from Charlie Amberson. Though she had read it earlier, she decided to look it over before falling asleep, with the hope that her friend's warm, rambling thoughts might drive some of the uneasiness from her own.

"*Henny, my love,*" the letter read. "*For once, something seems to be happening in my life to write to you about. It is not exactly paid employment, but I'm teaching my mother to ride. She's all hot for the outdoor life these days. Old Mrs. Curtayne, bless* her, lets us use her horses. Lucky I took all those riding lessons when my various daddies had money.

"Mother insists she's working on the great novel and I actually heard the typewriter going for about half an hour the other day.

"Last week, while she was out 'observing life,' I tried to sneak a real date with Old Sausage. (Junior is rather round, you must admit. Mother says he eats more groceries than he ever delivers.)

"Anyway, Sausage couldn't get the family car, so he scrubbed out the meat delivery truck and we tried a drive-in movie. It was a short evening. The whole van reeked of ground top round and sliced raw liver. Quelle smell!

"Maybe Provanza is not meant for me after all. But for some weird reason I just feel good around him. And Dallas likes him, doesn't he? They are sort of best friends, aren't they?

"And speaking of Dallas, two things to tell you: Mr. Engel from school stopped by Junior's store to ask for Dallas's address. Junior gave it to him. That's all right, isn't it? Maybe he's got a final math grade for him or something.

"Also, Junior told me that Dallas's father came by last week for a big sirloin steak and a bottle of Chianti — you know, that wine in the straw bottle everyone likes to put candles in. Sounds like a grand party, right? Junior said Mr. Dobson was a sharp dresser — western gear. Good-looking enough to be in the movies, even with that little limp. Junior said they didn't talk much about Dallas. You met his father once, didn't you? You never told me what you thought of him.

"In fact, old dear, why not call me up for a chat about this and whatever else is on your mind. I wouldn't dare run up a phone bill from this end. . . ."

She longed to speak with Charlotte, even to confide something about her concern over Dallas's recent moods and restlessness.

But it was after midnight in Thirty-nine Palms and that meant it was after three in the morning in Zenith. Retta switched off the bedside lamp and lay quietly, staring at the dark ceiling.

Though the house itself was still, Retta felt sure that in the master bedroom down the hall, her mother was also lying awake.

During breakfast, the day after Dallas and she had visited the church, Carter Caldwell had received a phone call. Later he packed a bag for a trip and caught a noontime plane from Palm Springs; he was still away.

For Henrietta, the Caldwell household never seemed quite at rest when her father was out of town. This was already his second trip east since they all left Zenith in the spring.

She fell asleep wondering about that phone call.

At midmorning next day, when Retta walked into the newsroom, her father signaled from his desk. She hurried to him and said in surprise, "I had no idea you were back in town."

"I was able to get a plane out of Philadelphia around midnight and cabbed right to the office from the airport. I knew your mother was scheduled for one of those Save the Trees meetings."

"Poppy, I could have met you."

"Well, we all seem to be in a rush these days. I wanted to save time."

"But you had a good trip, I hope?"

"Yes, Retta. Family business that needed to be looked into." He unsnapped the leather briefcase on his desk. "Fortunately, I took material with me and did some editing on the plane."

He took three typed, clipped pages from the briefcase. "Now, Retta, about your piece on St. Francis of the Rocks . . ."

She sank to the edge of a chair and waited. "I like what you did," her father said. "Fine observations, fine feelings. But it's more like an essay than a newspaper article."

"I can go back to interview the priest, quote him directly, if you like," Retta said.

"No need," he said, "though I must explain something to you. This is an interesting piece of work, but it takes special handling. I had *expected* a straight news story.

"In journalism, there are rules, Retta. A good reporter always tries for the kind of story the editor asks for. What if we'd been on a deadline?"

She felt her cheeks flush hot. "I'm sorry, Poppy. I've got a lot to learn. I know that."

"You're coming along," he said, "so don't worry about it too much right now. We're not *The New York Times*, are we? Just trying to be a good small-town paper.

"We can make use of your piece. I plan to run it next Saturday so it will be in readers' homes through the weekend. I'll assign a photographer to the church to get pictures."

She found herself smiling. "I'm so glad about this, Poppy. I was worried, almost scared. I thought I'd used too many words, too many adjectives, I mean."

"No," he said quickly, "though as I said, it's not the straight news article I expected. More of a mood piece, some nice touches of poetry."

She felt grateful but almost embarrassed. "Most of the words are mine," she said. "I mean, *I* decided how to put the sentences together, but it was Dallas who mentioned the birds were like prayers, flying into the sky like that. . . ."

"Dallas was with you?" he asked.

"Yes. It was his day off."

"Does he go to that church?"

"No. He doesn't belong to any particular church or religion."

Once again, her cheeks felt warm. She had meant to protect her feelings, to keep all fragile thoughts to herself, and yet it was she who had brought Dallas into the conversation and she who now had a strong need to defend him against any possible criticism.

"I just wish I could get to know your young man better," her father said. "You two always seem to be busy off somewhere else."

"But you know where we are," she answered quickly. "His workday at the Bradleys goes on till near bedtime. At night, I often help him with the chores. Otherwise, I would almost never get to see him."

"Perhaps the next time he's free, he might like to drive into town to have lunch with me," her father said. "Just the two of us."

"Oh, no!" she answered quickly. "Please don't ask him to do that, Poppy. He's shy. He likes you,

92

I know, but he's not exactly like us. He never really had a family except for his father and poor Sam Houston."

"I know about the brother who was killed some years ago," Retta's father said. "Your mother mentioned it to me back in Zenith. It must have been hard for Dallas and his father."

Retta nodded. "It's still hard for both of them," she said. "So much has been asked of Dallas. I mean, he's had so much responsibility in his life."

"All the more reason you should let us get to know him," her father said quietly. "I'm not pushing you, Retta. But it would be more fair to your mother and me."

"All right," she said tentatively. "We have until September. Can we just wait and see?"

Chapter
8

One weekend evening, since Mr. Bradley himself was at the ranch, Dallas was given an unexpected night off. When Retta drove to pick him up, he was in the bunkhouse, shower water still running.

Nathan Bradley came out of the barn, a long green lunge-line looped over his shoulder. He was a tall man, lean and wiry, with touches of gray in his hair and a crinkle of sun lines around his eyes. Retta had not seen him since last spring when she had asked the Bradleys to hire an unknown stable hand named Dallas Dobson.

Now Mr. Bradley called out, "Hello, there, Miss Caldwell. Good to see you. Dallas wants me to explain why he's so late." They shook hands and Retta could feel the strength in the man's fingers, the calloused toughness of his palm.

"We've got some excitement going on round here," Nathan Bradley said. "Dallas and I had some serious planning to do." He motioned Retta to a long bench running along the bunkhouse.

"It may not seem much to you, but Dallas was impressed," he said with a smile. "You see, there's a three-day rodeo coming to Danning soon. Danning is that little mountain town about thirty miles from here."

"I know about the Old West rodeo, Mr. Bradley. It runs from next Thursday through Saturday, doesn't it? Promoters put ads in our newspaper and there are posters on telephone poles along the roads."

"The big news," Mr. Bradley went on, "is that Fargo Haynes has agreed to be Grand Marshal. He'll open the rodeo on Thursday night. Fargo Haynes made a lot of fine western movies a number of years back. In my high school days, he was our hero."

"I've seen his movies on *The Late Show*," Retta said. "And I remember when he made those TV commericals for National Bank, the ones where he performed on a big white horse."

"That was his trick horse, Skeeter," Bradley explained. "That horse has an infected tendon right now, so he's out to pasture till it heals.

"Mr. Haynes called me from Hollywood a couple of hours ago. Never met the man myself, but he'd heard a lot about Rancho Arabian and asked if he could borrow a couple of horses for opening night. I told him we'd be honored. That's what Dallas and I've been talking about. We decided to lend him Moonbeam and Arista. I'm sure Arista's been trained to do everything Skeeter can do. My wife, the boy, and I will be in Scottsdale, but I'm sure Dallas can handle it. We'll get the Gomézes to stay on late here."

The screen door of the bunkhouse swung open and then bounced back, creaking on sunbaked hinges. Dallas stepped out, smelling of soap, his denim shirt spotted with water from pulling it on hastily after the shower.

"I've been telling your girl about the event in Danning," Mr. Bradley said. "I don't see why you can't take her along with you, Dallas."

"I'd love to go," Retta said quickly. "I'll help if I can."

"We'll both go, sir," Dallas said, speaking directly to Mr. Bradley. "And thanks for this extra time off. I'll call on Monday about those feed bills, then check with you in Scottsdale. Don't you and Mrs. Bradley worry about it."

"I've had no worries so far," Mr. Bradley said.

As they walked toward the car, Retta said, "Aren't you excited about the rodeo, Dallas? I am."

He shook his head. "I've got to take one thing at a time. A lot's going on these days." He patted his rear jeans pocket, then felt the pocket in his shirt.

"What's wrong? Have you lost something?" Retta asked.

"No. I have it. Now tell me, what is it you're supposed to do for the paper tonight?"

"I'll tell you while I drive," she said. "Here, you take the map."

The *Palms Gazette* was in the planning stages for a special edition to celebrate the local Date Ranchers Festival at the fairgrounds in October. Mr. Caldwell wanted Henrietta to start lining up ads.

"We'll have no trouble getting cooperation from the local merchants and probably every shop in the mall," she explained as they drove over a back road. "My father also wants ads from businesses back in the boondocks, for more western color. He likes to think the desert is still cowboy country, with a few shops and golf courses built around it."

She had the names of three back-country taverns to canvass that evening. The addresses had been checked and marked on a local map that lay across Dallas's knees. Retta glanced down at it.

"It didn't look this far on the map," she said. "Could we have passed it?"

Dallas rubbed the windshield with the back of his hand, but the obscuring haze was on the outside, a light blizzard of fine sand covering the glass. The grains were magnified, showing pink and dusty in the light of the setting sun.

He rolled down his window. On each side, the narrow lanes stretched off into a sea of rippling dunes. A wind snaked over the surface, blowing and shifting the low drifting sand as if it were sea fog.

"This road is almost eroded back to nature," Dallas said. "I don't see how a business could exist out here."

She continued driving for a few yards and suddenly, just behind a wind-stand of cottonwood trees, they saw a ramshackle building with a pair of weathered gas pumps in front and a rusted sign reading, CLINT'S PLACE.

"Looks like there's been nobody here for years," Dallas said.

97

"It was listed in the phone book," Retta said uncertainly. "Not the new one, an older one." Reaching into the backseat for the advertising order book, she added, "You wait in the car. I'll check to be sure."

She stepped out, shutting the door quickly. In this remote area, the desert wind was everywhere, changing directions and currents as it ruffled her hair and penetrated her light clothing. The moving air turned the surface of her skin into a damp sweat, then dried the moisture with the same hot breath.

Retta pulled her blouse tight around her throat against the stinging blow of sand and began to circle the tavern. Every window was shut tight, opaque with a coating of desert dust. Two doors had bolts, reinforced with closed padlocks. Retta stood a moment in this desolate, lonely space, listening to the creak of the swinging sign, the shifting, sighing noises of the winds. As she struggled back to the car, shoes filling with grit, her breath came short.

Dallas opened the door and pulled her in with a strong hand. "Make a tight U-turn right here," he said. "We'd better head back."

Retta turned slowly, carefully, to avoid sinking into the soft sand. She was relieved when she felt the traction of the tires on solid roadbed.

"Our next stop is the Bunking Bronco," she said in a tone of apology. "At least we'll get a decent welcome there."

"Maybe so, Retta, but remember it's Saturday night."

Retta cruised the crowded Bronco lot, looking for a parking space. Her headlights raked past dusty vans and cars, then hit the back of an open pickup truck, rousing two mongrel dogs huddled in sleep. The animals barked and growled fiercely at the yellow car for several moments, then sank back into slumber. Retta spotted a vacancy in the far corner of the lot.

"I'll go in with you," Dallas said.

"It will take me just a few minutes."

"I'll wait in a booth near the door," he insisted.

The Bunking Bronco seemed a different place this Saturday night. It was crowded with customers and the country and western music blaring from tapes was so loud it was like a pulsing, tangible thing. Both sound and people seemed to fill the room and push against the senses from all sides. Overhead lights were muted and cigarette smoke made a wispy second ceiling, floating low over the room.

Retta moved to one end of the bar, waving to attract the attention of the man she and Dallas had met here in early June. The proprietor saw her but before he could approach, someone at the bar pounded a beer glass, shouting for a refill. As the bartender moved off, Retta followed him, talking, trying to make herself heard above the music and the hum of human voices.

What happened next happened very quickly. Another glass was banged for a refill, then another and another. Most of the men lining the bar were young, Retta noticed, in their twenties and thirties. The group seemed friendly, even in high spirits, but caught up in a new game. The game was to keep the bartender busy moving from customer to customer, unable to talk to Retta, while she stood alone in front of the bar.

Determined not to look to Dallas for help, she

waited, watching the busy bartender, her cheeks pink with embarrassment.

The first man who had shouted for a refill jumped up suddenly, rushed to Retta, and scooped her up in his arms. A wave of laughter swept the smoky room.

The young man was strong and wiry, but he smelled of beer and his words slurred when he said, "You're gonna need help, little lady. Lemme give you a lift." He began to move along the bar. "Hey, wait up, Hank!" he shouted at the bartender. "The little lady here is trying to tell you something."

Underneath this seemingly good-natured teasing and flattery was a mood of drunken taunting and sexual belligerence.

Dallas left the booth by the door and stepped to the bar. "All right, fellow," he said without missing a beat. "Put her down. Miss Caldwell is just doing her job." His hands were motionless at his sides, but his eyes were unsmiling.

"We just want to help the young lady with her business," the drunken customer said.

"She can take care of her own business," Dallas said. "And I told you to put her down."

The bartender spoke up quietly but forcefully. "Do what the cowboy says, Johnson. He and his lady are considered friends at the Bronco."

The man set Retta carefully on her feet. He said tersely to Dallas, "Cowboy, we're not responsible for fillies turned loose around here."

Retta quickly tore an application blank from the order book and put it next to the cash register. "Please, Hank, read this, think it over," she called out to the proprietor. "The Date Ranchers Festival . . . it tells you right there how much the ads cost and where to send the money."

In the parking lot, Dallas said, "Give me the keys, Henrietta. I'd like to drive now."

As they pulled out onto the main road, the silence in the car was a mixture of resentment and controlled temper. Finally Dallas slapped his hand hard against the steering wheel.

"Your father is dead wrong, Retta," he said, "sending you out to business places like that at night. This isn't Zenith or Havendale High. Those guys back at the Bronco don't know you're one of the exalted Caldwells. And they couldn't care less."

"My father didn't tell me *when* to get those ads," she said. "I could have gone in the afternoon or even nine o'clock in the morning. I only decided to go tonight because you could come along."

He didn't speak again until the neon lights of the Cactus Corner, their next stop, were visible ahead through the dusty winds. "I may not always be around to stand up for you," he said with finality.

"What is *that* supposed to mean?" she asked, but Dallas had already swung into the parking lot and did not answer her directly.

"Just give me the ad book," he said. "I'll handle this one."

"*You'll* handle this one?" Retta said sharply. "What do you — "

"I'm sorry," Dallas interrupted. "That wasn't exactly what I meant to say."

He stepped from the car, pulled an envelope from his shirt pocket, and tossed it into Retta's lap. "I'm

101

tense tonight. I want you to do something for me," he said. "Read that letter, will you? It came this morning. It's meant for both of us, I think."

"Is it that important right now?" she asked. When he nodded, she reluctantly handed him the ad book without further comment.

Retta waited until he had disappeared into Cactus Corner, then slipped the letter from its envelope and leaned forward to read it in the light from the bar's outdoor sign.

The letter was neatly typed on stationery with the letterhead:

Mr. Edgar Engel, Mathematics Department
Havendale High School

The math teacher began by sending greetings to Dallas, then telling him that he, Engel, had recently had a meeting with the dean of admissions at Chester College, in East Chester, a Pennsylvania town about twenty miles from Zenith.

"I explained something of your background and told him of your work last year and Dean Ritter was impressed. He believes that if you earn the necessary credits and *diploma by January, as planned, he can guarantee you a scholarship for the freshman midyear semester at Chester College.*

"The scholarship would be renewable for four years, depending on performance. It includes a works-fund grant and the promise of a part-time job in your field. Chester College is near enough for you to commute as a day student. You could gain work experience and *money while on scholarship.*

"Dean Ritter asked me if you could handle basic science, agronomy, plus some other freshman

102

*courses in the veterinarian school, and I said I
thought so.*

*"You're a Texas cowboy at heart, Dallas, but I
think I got to know you pretty well at Havendale.
Your performance and determination convinced me
you are also a student. I don't see Dallas Dobson
as a day laborer on someone else's ranch for the
rest of his life. Can I tell the dean you're interested?"*

The letter was signed, *"Your friend, Edgar Engel,"*
in the teacher's familiar, precise handwriting.

Moments after Retta finished rereading it, Dallas
came back to the car and unlocked the door on his
side. "Cactus Corner will take a quarter-page ad,"
he said, handing Retta the ad book.

"That's great. Did you remind them to send in
their check?"

He pulled a small wad of currency from his jeans
and gave it to Retta. "I explained it good," he said,
"and the owner agreed to pay cash."

The letter from Mr. Engel was back in its envelope,
resting on the top of the dashboard. Neither mentioned the correspondence until the dark desert
road turned bright with the lights of Thirty-nine
Palms only a mile or so ahead.

Retta turned in the car seat so she could look
directly at Dallas. "I read the letter. Congratulations!
I feel so proud of you. You've told Mr. Engel yes,
haven't you?"

Dallas took a deep breath, then let it out in a
small explosion of frustration.

"God, Retta, sometimes you're impossible. The
letter just got here today. I barely had a chance to
read it when Mr. Bradley came up with the news
about the rodeo. How could I say yes?"

"I thought you might have phoned Mr. Engel right away," Retta said with exasperation.

"Don't you think I've got enough on my mind? How do you expect me to handle this, too?"

"I don't know why you're so angry, Dallas."

"Look. I'm just a two-bit cowhand from Texas. I'm already nineteen years old and I'm still trying to get out of high school. Now some teacher I hardly know is pressuring me to get even *more* schooling."

"But a college degree, Dallas . . . don't you want that?"

"Why are you leaning on me, Retta? Who says I can get something just because I want it? I haven't had a good, winning hand in life so far, have I?"

"Please," she said softly. "Talk to me so I can understand you. Are we having a terrible fight about something?"

He brushed his hand over his forehead once, roughly. "Yes, it's a fight, Retta. But I'm having it with myself. I guess you're out of it."

She felt him brake the car to pull off onto the shoulder of the road. He switched off the motor and lights, then rested both hands on the steering wheel, looking out into the desert darkness.

"Ever since I got Mr. Engel's letter, all the time I've been with you tonight, especially when I was in the Cactus and knew you were reading it, do you know what I hoped? In fact, what I *prayed* would happen?"

Retta shook her head. "What, Dallas?"

He sighed. "I hoped so hard I almost invented the words. When I got back to the car I wanted you to say, 'Dallas, the news is wonderful. Now you *know* you could get into Chester College if you wanted to.

Instead, forget about Mr. Engel and going back to Havendale High. Get the credits you need right here in Thirty-nine Palms. Anything — but *stay where I am*."

His tone was loud, hard with tension. "That's what I wanted you to say, Retta. That you wanted me in California."

His words echoed through her mind in jarring, splintered thoughts. She felt suddenly cornered by his vehemence and smoldering resentment.

"You're making me confused," Retta said, breathing in deeply. "You're way ahead of me. Everything seems upside down. The scholarship *seems* so right, I know going to college is right . . . how can I ask you to give all that up?"

"Right?" he asked sharply. "Can't someone be happy unless everything is *right?*"

"You said you were fighting with yourself," Retta replied, her voice trembling, "and you are. I can't say things you want to hear just because you want me to, Dallas."

He took the envelope from the dashboard, buttoned it with finality into his shirt pocket, then started the car and pulled back onto the highway.

With the window turned down on his side, desert winds scented with sagebrush drifted in and out. He drove slowly, sometimes no more than twenty miles an hour, seemingly determined to stretch out this time together, despite the unhappiness between them.

A half hour later, not far from the ranch, he said to her evenly, "I need something from you tonight, Retta and I'm not getting it. I thought that letter was about both of us. What we both want, what we both

105

feel. You don't seem to understand that. You're dumping this scholarship thing completely on me."

"I don't know why you're blaming *me*," she said. "You've had all day to think about what Mr. Engel wrote. I haven't. It's like you're using your anger against me to get out of making your own decisions."

He rolled up the window quickly, as if he had come to some conclusion, and accelerated speed. "Thanks. I think I got my answer," he said.

Just ahead the lights from the Bradley ranch reflected a faint glow into the dark sky. They both knew there would be no peaceful moments parked in the protection of the tall, dusty tamarisk trees that night.

Chapter
9

When the phone rang just before six the next morning, Retta felt weak with relief. She had waked early, trying to convince herself that Dallas would call, that he would not want to start a new day in anger.

But when she hurried to the foyer, belting her robe, her mother was already talking on the phone with her back to Retta. Her father stood nearby, listening, sipping a cup of coffee.

"No, no," her mother said, after listening for a few moments. "You were right to call us. It isn't something you should be embarrassed about. We'll send a check this morning by express mail." She listened again, then added, "No, of course not. No need to tell her anything at all."

Connie Caldwell hung up and spoke to her husband in a low voice. Retta was aware that her brother was standing beside her. They heard their father say, "She wouldn't ask for money if she didn't really need it. Three months behind . . . that's getting in deep. Make it a gift, Connie, not a loan. She can never pay it back. I'll try to see her when I get to Zenith this weekend."

"Back to Zenith!" Two whispered. "Every time we go one way, Pop goes the other. Like he kept flying out to California before he told us we had to leave Pennsylvania. Now this is his third trip back there."

When the phone rang a second time an hour later, Retta stayed in bed, staring at the sun-streaked ceiling until her mother called, "For you, Retta. Dallas . . ."

Retta picked up the hall phone and snaked the long cord out to the patio, closing the sliding glass door before saying hello.

"I'm talking from the barn," Dallas said in a whispering voice. "I don't want to cart feed to one more horse without talking to you, Retta."

"I can just barely hear you, Dallas." Retta clung to the phone.

"I don't want you to remember anything I said last night. I've got some thinking to do and I'll do it myself. But I need to be with you, right now, this morning."

"Aren't you working? Don't you have to get the horses ready for the rodeo tonight?"

"Yes, and you can help. The Bradleys left for Scottsdale but the Gomez guys are here. I'll be in town about eight-thirty to buy some things — hoof

108

polish, a curry brush. Can I pick you up to spend the day here?"

"If you can drive me back about three," she said. "I've got a column to finish for the paper."

"Then I'll see you soon."

"Dallas?" she spoke quickly, impetuously, almost before she realized what she meant to say.

"Yes?"

"I was so unhappy about last night. And about whatever part of it was my fault. Can you stay on the phone for a few moments more?"

"It's hard, Retta. In the daytime this is strictly a business phone."

"Just till you count to seventeen?" she asked. "A kind of prebirthday present for me?"

"Out loud?"

"No, to yourself. I'll count, too. Then we *both* hang up."

There was a silence at the other end of the line. Retta squinted her eyes against the morning sun, then glanced down at the smooth surface of the pool, pink and downy with cloud reflections. Her robe had fallen open and the direct rays of sun were warm on her neck and shoulder.

She held the telephone receiver close to her ear, lightly and delicately, aware of the healing silence that joined them. Just as she counted up to the number seventeen, the phone clicked down softly in the Bradley barn.

Retta was putting the last of the breakfast dishes away when her father came into the kitchen for a last cup of coffee. A truck rattled into the driveway beside the house. Moments later, the doorbell rang.

"I'll get it," Carter Caldwell said.

"It's Dallas," Retta told him. "I'm going out to the ranch for a while today."

"I'll tell him you'll only be a few minutes more," her father said.

But instead of the expected murmur of greetings at the front door, Retta heard her father's voice, loud and angry. "What in thunder is this all about?" were the only words she could make out.

She rushed to the foyer, but her mother and brother were there before her, crowded on either side of Carter Caldwell as he stood in the open doorway.

"What is it?" Retta cried out. "Let me see, too. Where is Dallas?"

Her brother stepped aside and Retta moved quickly past her parents to join Dallas on the doorstep. With a sharp intake of breath, she found herself gaping at a strange, surrealistic sight in the Caldwell's walled front garden.

The three-foot hedge of sprawling desert geraniums, the tall, spiny octillo bush with tatters of orange springtime blossoms still hanging from the thorns, the new twelve-foot palms, and even the giant saguaro cactus looked as if they had been caught in a summer snowstorm.

Every branch, prickly arm, or broad palm frond was hung, looped, draped, and festooned with long streamers of white toilet tissue — fresh, flimsy, and fragile, moving gracefully in the hot summer breeze.

"What does this mean?" Mr. Caldwell said in the

same stern voice. "Is this some kind of crazy California vandalism? I'm going to phone the sheriff's office and — "

"I don't think you need to, sir," Dallas said politely. "This isn't really vandalism. It's more a kid's trick, a grown-up kid. I've seen it done sometimes down in Texas. It's like a serenade or sending flowers. Guys do it at night to get someone's attention. It's to let everyone in the neighborhood know a pretty girl lives in this house. It's meant to be a compliment."

"But *how* do they do it? And *why* do they do it?" Mr. Caldwell asked.

"Somebody, or a group of guys more likely, knows Retta moved in here," Dallas said. "It's easy to decorate a yard like this. You just keep throwing rolls of toilet tissue up into the branches. Some of it catches on, the rest of the roll falls to the ground. You just throw it up over and over again till the roll's used up."

Carter Caldwell still looked annoyed, but his voice had calmed. "Do you know who would do this, Retta?" he asked.

She shook her head. "I don't know anyone special here in Thirty-nine Palms except Dallas and the Bradleys. And the staff down at the *Gazette*."

Two groaned and slapped a hand against his cheek in mock concern. "I think I know, Retta. In the mall that day a while ago, when you were doing a story for the paper and I passed you on the escalator, remember?" Retta nodded.

"Well," her brother said, "when you waved to me, a couple of guys asked me who the pretty girl was and I said you were my sister. They live in Thirty-nine Palms, too. They told me they would be seniors at the new high school this fall. I told them you were enrolled there."

"You didn't give your sister's address to a couple of strangers, did you?" Mr. Caldwell asked. "I hope you have more sense than that, Two."

"Of course I didn't do that," Two said quickly. "I just introduced myself. I told them I was Carter Caldwell, Jr., and we shook hands, that's all."

Mrs. Caldwell put her arm around her daughter's shoulder. "That explains it, dear," she said to her husband. "We *are* the only Carter Caldwells here. It would be easy to find out where we live. I don't think this should be taken too seriously. As Dallas pointed out, it *is* meant to be a compliment."

"I don't like it," Mr. Caldwell said firmly. "I think it's unsightly, a public nuisance, and an invasion of privacy. It seems to me that Two definitely lacks a certain — "

Dallas cut in hastily. "Let me clean it up for you, sir. I'll need a ladder for the palm trees and the saguaro. Is there one in the garage?"

"I'll get it for you," Two said, hurrying toward the garage before his father could speak again.

Some time later, working at top speed, Dallas and the two younger Caldwells had the trees, cacti, and geranium hedges almost stripped and picked clean of the white paper ribbons. Mr. Caldwell and his wife had left earlier for the office.

Dallas stood balanced on the top rung of the ladder, one hand clutching firmly at the rough bark of a palm tree, reaching far above him to grasp the last wisps of paper. As he stretched, then pulled, lengths

112

of toilet tissue came loose and floated to the ground.

Two had gathered the entire mass of material into one huge heap of fluffy paper piled in the middle of the small lawn. Amused and excited, he looked at the snowy accumulation with admiration.

"Gee, Retta," he said, "those guys gotta think a lot of you. This must have been at least an eight-roll job."

At first glimpse that morning, the festooned trees and other plants had looked beautiful to Retta, like an apple orchard burst into bloom overnight. But while they worked to clean up, she became aware of a change in Dallas's manner. As minutes ticked by, he seemed to lose the look of warmth and animation she had been so pleased to see when they first stood on the doorstep together.

Two spoke up unexpectedly. "I hope it's the big blond one who calls you first, Retta. He plays basketball, he told me. Probably one of the top guys in the senior class."

Suddenly Retta knew exactly what had changed the mood on this important, sunny morning.

"Two," she said sharply, "do you *know* what you're saying? I'm beginning to agree with Poppy. You do lack a certain something in your personality, and I think it's *tact*."

"But, Retta," he persisted, "you and the guys will be in the same school and everything. It's natural. I mean, Dallas has to go back — "

"Sometimes I can't believe you're really my brother," Retta said forcefully. "You're making me very angry. If I were Poppy, I'd have made you clean up this mess by yourself. You caused it. I don't see why it has anything to do with me at all. I haven't even *met* those people yet. . . ."

"That 'kid's trick' took longer to clean up than I expected it would," Dallas said.

"Sorry about that, Dallas." Retta looked at him for a moment.

Those were the only words spoken on the trip back to Rancho Arabian. The pickup truck had no air-conditioning so that the air that flowed through the open windows was already heavy and warm, at least ninety-five degrees, Retta guessed, working up toward the inevitable searing heat of an August day.

Dallas glanced at his watch twice, then accelerated the truck to top legal speed, his eyes intent on the dusty road. But once at the ranch, he was vocal, matter-of-fact.

"Here's how we'll work today," he said. "All the stock has been fed and watered for now. The Gomezes already did a good barn and corral cleanup. You and I will make Estrella comfortable now. We won't have that extra hour this evening. Then we spend time on the horses we're taking to the rodeo tonight."

He led the pregnant mare from her stall and tethered her in the shade of a jacaranda tree. The horse's silver-gray coat was already damp and dark with sweat.

When the bathing, toweling, and brushing were completed, Dallas swept up the long, silky mane and pinned it up off the horse's back with a series of plastic clothespins.

"That should be cooler, old girl," he said. He

began moving his hand carefully over the mare's taut belly.

Retta saw him frown. "Is something the matter?" she said.

"I'm not sure." He put his cheek tight against the gray, shining hide as if listening, trying to divine what might be going on with the new life inside. He lightly massaged the horse again. "That foal seems to have changed position since yesterday. It's farther back than I expected."

"Should you call Scottsdale? Should you tell the Bradleys?" she asked.

He shook his head. "Mr. Bradley told me Dr. Meacham was out last night looking over the stock when I was with you. He checked Estrella and said everything was A-okay. So I won't worry."

He untied the lead line and began to walk the mare back to the barn. "These hundred-and-fifteen-degree days are murder on a pregnant animal," he said.

"Maybe you can put extra straw in her stall," Retta suggested. "Get her to lie down."

Dallas answered with a short laugh. "Estrella is a stand-up horse. She likes to sleep on all four legs. She'll know when she needs to lie down. That will mean she's ready to give birth."

It was high noon when Dallas led the show horses out to the sunlit courtyard for grooming. Retta made several trips to the barn for warm water. The exertion, the weight of the swinging buckets, hurt her hands and sent trickles of sweat running down between her shoulder blades.

They worked side by side but separately. Dallas selected Arista to bathe and Retta took Moonbeam, working in silence until the horses stood fresh and clean, hides steaming in the hot desert air.

Retta tossed the buckets of sudsy water out over the mint bed at one side of the barn. "Aunt Blue taught me to do that," she called out to Dallas. "It works with roses, too. Cleans off the dust, and the soap is like a fertilizer."

He did not seem to hear. Out of the locked vault in the barn, he had carried a long wooden box and was unpacking items onto a bench. From layers of blue packing paper, he removed pairs of ribboned rosettes to decorate the horses' manes, and cascading clusters of ribbons in the red, black, and gray colors of Rancho Arabian to tie at the upper base of each high, flaunting tail.

"Can I help you with those things?"

"No, I'm just checking them," he said. "They don't go on until Danning." Then he added, "The hoof work is next. I do that myself. I'll get the stuff from the tack room while you refill the buckets. Hotter water this time, Retta."

She glanced up at the sun. It was almost directly above them, a burning white orb, so intense, so bright that even a glance dried the moisture on her eyeballs.

At a faucet inside the barn, she cupped her hands for water and sipped it slowly, letting the moisture ease over her dry mouth and throat. But it tasted brackish, like old tea, and she spat the tepid liquid out into the sink.

In the courtyard Dallas had knotted a bandanna

116

around his forehead to keep sweat out of his eyes, and his work shirt was dark with perspiration. He knelt on the sandy ground, close to Arista's front hooves, sorting equipment. Retta set down the buckets within his reach.

From a work basket, he selected a pair of brushes, a pumice buffer, two metal hoof picks, the polish he had bought earlier that day, and a roll of toilet tissue, still in its outer wrappings.

Retta felt a spasm of apprehension at the sight of the paper. "Toilet tissue!" she said. "I thought we all had enough of that for one day. What do you want it for now?"

Dallas rocked back on his heels and said quietly, "Horse groomers use tissue for buffing. It's the last step, the final hoof polish."

He looked at her directly. "Stand back, will you, Retta? I don't want you behind the horses while I'm working. In fact, you're in my way."

Stunned by his words, she stepped back, just inside the shadows of the barn. For almost an hour she watched as he scrubbed hooves and forelocks, then worked over each hoof again, probing and picking to remove pebbles and matted straw.

He was hot, sweating profusely, but he seemed determined not to stop or ask for water. It was more than a physical discomfort, she knew, that etched his face with such unhappiness and brought spots of color to his cheekbones. The single roll of toilet tissue had rekindled the same baffled, angry emotions she had seen that morning.

Dallas went down on his knees, his back deliberately turned toward the barn, and began to shine one of Arista's front hooves. The heavy, slapping sounds seemed to accentuate the web of silence that hung between them.

Retta felt she couldn't stand the punishing isolation any longer. She stepped into the sunlight. "Dallas, I want you to stop working on those horses and *talk* to me."

"Not now," he said coldly. "It's the wrong time. I wouldn't know what to say."

She moved closer and took off her sunglasses so he would have to look directly into her eyes. "I want you to look at me, Dallas. I think you're angry because of that silly paper thing that happened at my house this morning. You're all worked up over people I've never even met. . . ."

Dallas stood suddenly and looked at her, his eyes so direct, so gray-green and intent that it was she who flinched and averted her gaze.

"You're forgetting one important word you used this morning, Retta. You said '*yet*.' 'I haven't met those people *yet*.' In front of your brother — even now — you don't want to come out and admit it, do you?"

"Admit what, Dallas? What are you talking about?"

"That you are planning to go out with other guys when I'm gone. You are, aren't you? As soon as school starts, probably. You're even thinking about it *now*, while I'm still in California."

"Stop it!" Retta said loudly. "I haven't thought about that *at all*. You're not being fair. Why do you want me to feel guilty about something that hasn't even happened?"

"But it will," he said flatly. "You said *yet*. You haven't met those guys *yet*. . . ."

118

He pulled the wad of tissue paper off his fist and stuffed it into the work basket. "In case you're wondering, Miss Caldwell, yes, we *are* having a fight and this time we're both in it. And yes, I *am* jealous. It hit me hard at your house this morning. I'm jealous of you and it hurts. I don't think you even care about that."

His voice was low, almost gruff. "Ask one of the Gomez guys to drive you home. Do whatever you have to do, but come back here by seven. With two horses, I'll really need you tonight to get to the rodeo."

"Dallas," she said, "let me say something. If you weren't so emotional — "

He turned quickly and put his face against the great, warm curve of Arista's shoulder and tangled both hands in the mare's thick, silver mane.

"Go away," he mumbled. "Please, just go away."

The desert sun was still bright as Retta stood to one side, watching Dallas load the two valuable Arabians. He tethered them a foot apart inside the van, soothing them with words and gentle handling.

The traffic on the main highway leading to the mountain town of Danning was heavy, and Dallas drove carefully and at even speed. His concentration made it easy for them both to avoid conversation, and even with the heavy van and steep climb, the drive took little more than half an hour.

Finally, at the far end of a rutted road leading into the rodeo site, Retta could see a shafted cone of light reaching into the dark sky and hear the rolling sound of crowds and country music.

Dallas drove slowly, scanning the hand-lettered

signs nailed to trees and fence posts that gave directions to individual corrals and parked trailers.

When the headlights hit a plyboard arrow printed with the name Fargo Haynes, he turned the van in that direction into a clearing of trampled grass, an expensive house trailer parked at the far edge.

When they both stepped down from the cab, Dallas locked the rig securely, turned to Retta and put an impersonal hand on her shoulder. "We're about twenty minutes early for Haynes," he said. "Let's look around."

The rodeo was located in a small country fairgrounds with a large center show ring surrounded by tiers of rickety red bleachers. In the background was a fringe of rough cement-block stables and outbuildings.

Spotlights rigged on high poles brightened the center ring, but the rest of the rural grounds was dimly lit, mostly by headlights from parked cars and vans and strings of colored lights strung from tree to tree. At one side of the grounds there were rows of booths — small, open-faced structures built of weathered wood and roofed with dry, rustling palm fronds.

Retta breathed deeply, feeling the stringent brace of clean, high air in her lungs. The new town of Thirty-nine Palms was built on the desert floor but Danning, an old stagecoach stop, was three thousand feet above that base. The atmosphere here was crisp and cool, the sky dotted with bright stars, making a strong illumination that touched the rim of dark mountain peaks rising in the background.

It could have been the stimulus of the crowd or the abrupt change in altitude, but Retta felt suddenly light-headed, giddy with excitement.

"Oh, Dallas," she said, ignoring the strain between them. "It's so beautiful, so *make-believe*. It's like a circus."

"I can show you more," he said. "It was like this in Texas."

For a time they drifted with the crowd, caught up in the closeness of bodies, the human babble, and the rhythms of country music sounding from the loudspeakers. The air was scented with grilling hamburgers, popcorn, keg beer, and the sweet, oily smell of fresh Indian fry bread. Over the whole scene, lifted by the mountain breeze, was the hot animal smell of horses and fresh, sharp manure.

Dallas walked so fast, with such a sense of urgency, that Retta could barely keep up with him as he strode past rows of stands displaying fancy lariats, shiny belt buckles, and burnished Texas leathers.

"Retta, can I buy you something?" Dallas asked unexpectedly.

After the searing tensions of the last hours, she was startled by the warmth of his voice. "No. I mean . . . not right now, but thanks," she said.

Dallas had stopped at the last booth, a structure so far at the end of the row that it was barely visible in the twinkle of strung-out lights.

Retta was aware of a tinny, *tick-tick* noise. She saw that a lone woman in the booth was winding up small mechanical bucking broncos with brown and white markings, setting the toy animals out on the wooden counter to buck, toss, and tumble. When one stopped moving, she wound it again and set it back with the herd.

121

"Wanna buy one?" the woman asked, her voice soft with a Texas drawl. "No batteries, just windup. Only two dollars."

Retta waited for Dallas to speak but he was silent, studying the woman with open curiosity. "We really came up here to deliver some horses," Retta heard herself say.

"Just try the little critters for fun, then," the old woman said. "Your gentleman, too."

At closer range, the lady was not as old as she first appeared, Retta realized, maybe thirty-five or thirty-six, and almost girlish in a short western outfit of white fringed buckskin and a Texas hat. Even her face was young-old, round and soft, but heavy with makeup, false eyelashes, and blue eyeshadow. Her bleached blonde hair hung in braids tied with leather thongs.

"Here," she said to Dallas. "Let me put one of these little fellas out where you can see it." She picked up a bronco and stepped out into the pathway in front of the booth.

Retta saw now that the woman was pregnant, the small, rounded curve of her stomach pulling the hem of her skirt high above the ornate white boots. She sighed lightly as she bent over to put the windup bronco on the flattened grass. The miniature horse bucked, tumbled, and tossed like a real-life bronco until its movements began to unwind into slow motion.

Then the woman picked up the toy and held it out to Retta, the brown metal legs still kicking feebly on the palm of her outstretched hand.

"Any kids at home?" she asked. "You two got any little cowboys?"

Retta was aware that Dallas had turned toward her and was watching her intently. Unable to decide what to say, she simply shook her head.

"Come on, honey," the woman urged. "Take the bronc. It's a gift. You're gonna have kids someday."

"I just couldn't . . ." Retta began, but Dallas stepped forward and reached out for the windup bronco.

"That's right nice of you, ma'am," he said. "I'll take it for my girlfriend." He unbuttoned his shirt pocket and put the toy inside. Then he touched his forehead with one hand, as if he were doffing a hat. The woman smiled at him.

"I'll see that some kid gets this," he said then. "And thank you kindly, ma'am. We sure appreciate it."

As they zigzagged back through the crowds toward Fargo Haynes's house trailer, Retta saw Dallas glance back once, but the blonde lady was not looking after them. She was standing alone in the booth, still winding and unwinding the toy broncos.

"Did you know that woman? Have you seen her before?" Retta asked. Dallas shook his head. "Then I don't understand," she said. "Why did she want to give us a gift?"

Dallas shrugged. "Lots of country folk have big hearts."

He laughed but without real warmth. "Funny I should say something like that. It's what my father always said about *his* ladies: '. . . *hearts as big as all Texas*.' He ought to know, I guess."

Retta waited near the van while Dallas walked to Fargo Haynes's luxurious house trailer to introduce himself and to ask Haynes to inspect the horses.

At this distance from the show ring, an announcer's voice was a wordless, booming echo. Country music floated up thin and tinkling against the backdrop of trees and mountains. Behind her, Retta could hear the occasional thud of hooves and the weighty, shifting noise as the horses' great bodies brushed against the inside of the van.

After a long wait, she finally heard Dallas call to get her attention and saw him hurrying down the path from Haynes's trailer. He was alone and carrying two pails of water.

"Let's get the horses out," he said. "We're going to meet Haynes at the entrance to the ring."

"Doesn't he want to look them over first?"

Dallas shook his head as he unlocked the rear door of the van. "He didn't even want to see me. He brought a couple of guys down with him from Hollywood. They're up there drinking and playing cards. Haynes is sleeping, they told me, but they'll have him at the show gate in five minutes."

Dallas walked Arista down the ramp, talking to her softly before handing the reins to Retta. Then he swung back to release Moonbeam.

While both horses drank thirstily, Dallas pinned the colorful rosettes in their manes and festooned the arch of their tails with the bright red, black, and gray ribbons.

Then, as Retta held both bridles, he pulled the red bandanna from his own forehead, and refolded and retied it. He tightened his belt a notch, ran a hard hand down each leg of his jeans, tucking the narrow folds into his boot tops. Reaching into the van, he took out an American flag rolled smoothly

124

around a short staff. With the flag in one hand and Arista's lead in the other, he said, "Let's go, Retta."

Nearly ten minutes passed before Fargo Haynes appeared at the corral near the show ring. There was a spatter of applause as some of the barn hands recognized the old star, but Haynes did not seem to hear. He had one hand on a companion's shoulder, while using the other to steady himself on a corral rail as they walked toward the show gate.

Haynes was a big man, the two young people saw, more than six feet tall, broad-shouldered, with long white hair and a weathered face as brown and lined as desert hardpan. He was dressed for a starring role, in buckskin and a Texas broadbrim, his neck and wrists decorated with heavy turquoise-and-silver Indian jewelry that sent out flashes of light. Even though it was nighttime, Haynes wore large, square sunglasses that covered not only his eyes but nearly a third of his broad, ruddy face.

He paused for a moment, as though he were out of breath, then took a hand from the corral fence to wipe his mouth. Without that support, he sagged suddenly and his companion hastened to steady the big man.

Haynes seemed to see Retta, Dallas, and the horses for the first time. He shook his head sharply before saying, with real admiration, "Good-looking horseflesh." Then, with a look at Retta, "And good-looking filly."

She was aware then of the sharp, acrid reek of whiskey.

"Thank you, sir," Dallas said politely, while keeping the reins of both horses firmly in his hands.

Haynes's companion spoke up. "Now, young

man, as your boss explained it on the phone, you're going to lead out on the second-string horse, and ride twice around the ring, holding the American flag.

"Second time round, when you pass this gate, Haynes comes out on the trick horse. You both circle the ring a couple times together, you exit. Fargo goes front and center, slacks up on the reins, and lets Arista go through her tricks. Fargo takes his bows."

"You got it almost right, sir," Dallas said, "but there are some changes. *I* ride the trick horse tonight. Mr. Haynes and I go out side by side, real close. I'll have a lead line between Arista and Moonbeam. We'll circle the ring twice." He turned to the old cowboy. "I'll be controlling both horses, Mr. Haynes. You just concentrate on keeping your seat."

As Fargo Haynes stepped forward, his face a deeper shade of red, Dallas held up his hand. "That's the way it's going to be. I'll have the flag *and* the trick horse. My girl will be waiting at the gate here to take Moonbeam's lead line, maybe help Mr. Haynes dismount. Arista and I go front and center."

Haynes's deep voice came out in an explosion of indignation but the words were slurred, almost liquid. "Those folk out there came to see *the* Fargo Haynes, not some two-bit cowpunk. What's this all about, boy? Are you suggesting Fargo Haynes is too drunk to do his job? You think I can't ride any horse alive?"

"I'm not trying to insult you, sir," Dallas said, "but I do know something about drinking. You're not

126

going to hurt yourself or this horse tonight. I take full responsibility for what we're going to do, Mr. Haynes. I'll explain to my boss."

Haynes stood silent. He was no taller than Dallas but with his bulk, show business costume, and glittering jewelry, he seemed the dominant figure, making Dobson seem light and slim as a young boy.

For several moments, no one moved or spoke. Then Dallas said, "Excuse me, sir," and reached over to remove Haynes's dark glasses. He handed them to Henrietta, saying, "Hold them for him, will you? The crowd out there came to see Fargo Haynes — all of him."

Without glasses, the old cowboy seemed defenseless, almost vulnerable. His eyes were a bright, watery blue, the white crisscrossed with tiny, red veins. He squinted closely at Dallas for several seconds, blinking rapidly, as if his eyeballs hurt.

"All right, Dobson," he said. "We'll try it your way."

Dallas waited until the Hollywood crony had helped Fargo Haynes into the saddle. Then he laid Moonbeam's reins in the old man's right hand and guided his left till it clenched tightly on the pommel of the saddle. Dallas pulled the cinch rein tight, tethering it to Arista's saddle where he could control it. Then he mounted the trick horse and stuck the base of the short flagpole firmly into the leather cup on the horse's saddle.

Haynes spoke up suddenly, his words hard and clear. "You've got some *macho*, cowboy. You better damned well know how to ride."

A rodeo employee gave a hand signal toward the broadcaster's booth, then swung the gates open into the show ring.

The announcer shouted out, "Ladies and gentlemen, here's what we've all been waiting for! That celebrated western megastar, the great Fargo Haynes and his sidekick, Dallas Dobson! Plus those famous Arabian prize horses, Moonbeam and the incomparable Arista!"

The music of the *William Tell* overture sounded from the loudspeakers and a murmur of expectancy moved through the crowd.

Dobson and Haynes left the gate together, Dobson and Arista on the outside, with the actor and Moonbeam on the inside. Under the younger man's guidance, Arista began to move out in a wide, graceful circle, leading Moonbeam and the old cowboy around with her, linked by the connecting line.

As the horses' speed increased, the flag began to unfurl slowly. There was applause, then stomping and whistling as the riders came into the center of the ring. Spotlights mounted on high poles cast circles of light over Dobson and the stocky, flamboyant figure of Fargo Haynes.

Second time around the ring, Dallas urged Arista into a brisk trot. He rode closer to Haynes, almost shoulder to shoulder now, ready to prod him back if he slipped in the saddle. But the older man had begun to react to the approval of the crowd, sitting tall, letting his body move easily with the movement of the horse. Haynes shook his head, as if to clear his thoughts, then — holding the pommel firmly in one hand — swept off his big white hat to wave and salute the crowd.

128

At the exit gate, Retta found herself jumping up and down, clapping her hands in wild applause. Dallas picked up the pace, going into a medium canter so the horses' manes and high tails flowed in the breeze and the American flag came unfurled.

No one in that audience could guess that the cowboy star, now beaming, so charismatic, only moments before had been stunned and nearly speechless with liquor, unable to walk by himself.

As the horses finished a third circle of the ring and approached the exit gate, Dallas reined in and swung round so he could hand the flag, staff-end first, to Retta and then toss her the cinch lines. Awkwardly, yet careful not to let the loose folds of cloth touch the ground, Retta tucked the flag under one arm and began to lead Moonbeam, Haynes still in the saddle, back inside the corral.

From the ring, she heard the announcer's voice say, "And let us welcome once again the famous Arista, ridden by Dallas Dobson of Rancho Arabian!"

Retta longed to rush back to the gate to watch, but instead waited patiently, holding Moonbeam by the bridle, while the man from Hollywood helped Fargo Haynes to make a slow, sliding dismount. Haynes was panting, as if short of breath. When Retta handed him his dark glasses, he nodded, without looking at her, then moved back to the gate to watch the action in the ring.

Retta led Moonbeam to one end of the corral and tethered her to a rail. She could hear the sound of applause and quickly worked her way back to the gate, still carrying the flag.

Out in the spotlight, the great silver Arabian stood tall and muscled, her arched and elegant neck quivering with response to the loud applause. Dallas sat easy in the saddle, holding the reins lightly. He had been guiding the trick horse through her paces, Retta guessed, with the subtle inner pressure of his knees.

Now, at the rider's silent command, Arista reared and began to walk, almost upright on her hind legs, in a small, sedate circle, a graceful equine aristocrat turning to face every section of the tiered arena before coming to a halt.

At a new knee-nudged instruction, the horse went into the finale of her performance. Bending forelegs to the ground in a kneeling curtsy, Arista touched her silvery forelocks to the ground in a farewell bow. Horse and rider held the pose for several long seconds while the crowd hooted and applauded in appreciation.

Dallas reined the horse back to a standing position, then guided her backward toward the exit gate, the horse taking mincing, intricate steps. The announcer shouted out, "Let's hear it for Arista and Dallas Dobson!" and the crowd clapped wildly until the pair was out of sight inside the corral.

By the time Dallas had dismounted, Fargo Haynes and his Hollywood friend were already at the end of the muddy lane, turning off the path toward the house trailer.

Chapter 10

B ack at the horse van, Dallas doused his flushed face with water, massaging the back of his neck with the cold liquid before fetching fresh buckets for the horses.

As they drank, he stripped both Arabians of saddles and other gear. Retta grabbed a towel and began to rub down Arista's shining flanks while Dallas turned to Moonbeam.

"They're both heated up pretty bad," he said. "Especially Arista. We'll hot-walk them for twenty minutes now. When we get to the ranch, I'll sponge them down and walk them again."

Later, when the horses were vanned, Retta said, "Can't we rest a few minutes before starting back?

You were so good back there, Dallas. I never knew you could handle a horse that way."

"Let's talk while we drive," he said. As she slid into the passenger seat, he added, "Give me about five minutes. I'll try to square things with Mr. Haynes."

"Don't you want me to go with you? Wouldn't that be best?"

"No," he said firmly. "If he's going to shout or curse, I don't want you there. You can't tell how drunks will act."

Retta listened as his footsteps crunched away in the darkness. Then she rested her head on the cool leather seat, shut her eyes, and tried to relax, but her thoughts were so alive, so energized by the events of the evening that she could hear imaginary applause and almost see Dallas and the great silver mare, strutting and bowing in the spotlight.

Some time later, she wakened with a start as Dallas pulled out of the rutted rodeo grounds and onto the main highway. Feeling disoriented, somehow cheated, she was aware of the mountain coolness on the night breeze, the last melancholy strains of country music growing fainter as they left the fairground scene behind.

"You must have been gone so *long*, Dallas," she said in a half whisper. "How could I fall asleep? What happened back there? What did Fargo Haynes say?"

"Not much," Dallas answered, eyes intent on the dark stretch of highway ahead. "But he told me he'd decided to stay on till Saturday. That's the last night of the rodeo."

"That's it? That's all you talked about?"

"Except for a few odds and ends. He's originally from Texas. We talked some about that. He thought maybe he'd met my father down there, and even Sam Houston, but he wasn't sure."

She waited, watching Dallas's face as it was reflected dimly in the windshield — thoughtful, almost sad. It was a private look, the familiar guarded expression she remembered. It had crossed his face every time his father was mentioned back in those first days in Pennsylvania.

Retta had met Daniel Dobson only once, on a dark, chilly afternoon when classes at Havendale High had been dismissed early so the faculty could go to a county teachers' meeting. Dallas had asked her for a lift home.

Neither she nor Dallas had expected his father to be there in the midafternoon, but he was. As they stood together in the cold, shabby front room, they both heard movement upstairs. Moments later, Danny Dobson hobbled down on crutches, his face stiffly angry, his breath touched with the rancid smell of stale liquor. He had been a shock to them both — rude, belligerent, and openly resentful of Retta's presence.

It had been a short time later, that same afternoon when they were ready to part, that Retta felt the full trauma of Dallas's troubled relationship with his father. Before she could drive away, he leaned on the open window of her car and held her hand so tightly that her bones hurt and she could feel the pulse of blood in his veins.

It was an emotional moment, one she recalled

133

vividly, an interlude when she and Dallas came to understand each other. And it had been perhaps the first time Retta was willing to admit their interdependence.

"No matter what you think, Retta," he had said that cold afternoon, "I still love him. I'll always love him. He's part of whatever I am. He could have given me away but he chose not to. He wanted two sons. I'll always remember that."

Now, driving through the night away from the rodeo, Dallas seemed to change his mood deliberately, with conscious effort. He leaned forward to tune the radio to some faraway music, turning up the volume to catch the wispy threads of sound that came and went, as if straining to travel the airways over the dark, high mountains.

He held the steering wheel loosely in one hand, beating time to the music with the other. "By the way," he said, "Mr. Haynes said to tell you good-bye and thanks for helping out tonight. He seems to think you're quite a girl."

His profile showed clean and sharp in the reflection from the dashboard but Retta saw a distinct frown marking his forehead. When he did not look at her, she sensed his thoughts were far away. He was not thinking about her at all.

Within ten minutes, they were out on the main highway, beginning a descent from the mountain heights to the distant valley plateau of Thirty-nine Palms and outlying Rancho Arabian. At first the horse van was part of a stream of traffic from the rodeo. Then, one by one, cars turned off to single roadside homes, trailer parks huddled against dusty windbreaks, or journeyed on toward ranches far off the road.

By the time their vehicle began to travel past the boundaries of the Norongo Indian Reservation, Dallas and Retta had the highway almost to themselves.

He moved up to a constant 55 miles an hour, then rolled down his window. Already the night air had begun to warm as they left the cooler mountain temperatures for the blast-furnace heat of the valley below.

The headlights of the van cut brilliant shafts through the night ahead, but on either side of the highway the land looked deserted, stretching out black and silent. Retta tried to accustom her eyes to penetrate the dark, but she could barely make out the gray stretches of stony fields, scraggly creosote bushes, and a few dwarf pines — an opaque backdrop with some shape and depth but with an almost total absence of color. Those bleak foothills were, Retta knew, home to what was left of the Norongo Indian tribe.

She moved closer to Dallas, needing the reassuring comfort of his nearness, then gestured toward the black landscape.

"It looks so deserted, so lonely. You would never guess there werc real, breathing people still living back there." Dallas glanced quickly out his window.

"My father wants to run a history of the Norongos in the paper around Thanksgiving," she went on. "There are only about two hundred people left on this reservation now. In the old days, before the white man, there were lots — whole families. No

135

alcohol, no drugs, plenty of work. A seed-gathering tribe, following the old ways."

Dallas reached to turn the volume down on the radio till the jazz background was no more than a musical blur. When he turned to speak, he seemed to have heard nothing of what she'd just said. His query took her completely by surprise.

"Henrietta, why didn't you like that lady back there?"

"What lady, Dallas?"

"The blonde, the lady in the cowboy outfit."

"You mean the one that gave you the little bronco?"

"Yes, that lady. She was trying to be nice to you. I could tell by the way she smiled. Why didn't you want to buy something, Retta?"

"First of all, I *did* like her," Retta protested. "I just didn't want to buy a toy. I have no use for it. . . ."

"You could have *pretended* you had a kid at home when she asked you. You could have bought one for your brother."

"Why me? You didn't buy anything, either," she said defensively. "In fact, no one at the rodeo seemed to want those broncos."

"That's why it was important," he said. "She'd got herself dressed up, makeup and all. I'm sure she's not from Danning or Thirty-nine Palms. She probably came a long way from somewhere. That's why I wish you'd been nicer to her."

"Why didn't you say something back there?" Retta said.

"I hoped it would be a natural, spontaneous thing," he answered quietly. "That you'd *want* to

136

have a conversation with her. It wouldn't have hurt you to let that lady think you had a little cowboy at home. . . ."

"Little cowboy . . ." As she heard them, those two words stood out suddenly for Retta as if they had been caught in a spotlight of significance. She remembered last November, a night they had sat alone together for the first time in her car on a dark road in Pennsylvania.

He needed to talk to her, he had said. *I think we're going to be more than friends, Henrietta. So there are things you should know about me, things I want to tell you myself.*

He had told her, that chill night, that his father had never married the blonde, bright-faced teenaged rodeo clown he had met while touring in Texas. That girl had just turned seventeen years old when she gave birth to a baby boy in a clinic in Waco, Texas.

"My mother was just a kid," Dallas had repeated insistently that first evening. "I don't really blame her for being scared to keep me, but I was with her that whole first day at the clinic. She wanted to hold me, kind of memorize what I looked like, my father told me. If we'd stayed a family, she'd have liked me, I always felt that."

On the same aching, bittersweet night, she had heard him say these words: "I often imagined that if she'd had a nickname for me, it might be 'little cowboy,' or something like that."

Glancing at him now as they sped down the mountain, she searched her mind for the healing words she wanted so much to say. When she did speak, her voice was soft and persuasive, almost as if she were talking to a child.

"Let me ask you something, Dallas. What's troubling you right now, it's really more about *you* than *me*, isn't it? I'd like to talk about it, but you'll have to help. . . ."

He looked at her quizzically. "Help? Help with *what?*"

"Help with remembering," she said. "I don't want to guess. I don't want to try counting it out on my fingers. You just tell me. How old is your mother right now?"

He laughed sharply. "What a question! What made you think of asking something like that?"

"You know — blonde hair, lots of makeup, Texas accent, still likes to be around horse people," she said.

"There are a lot of rodeo groupies with blonde hair and makeup who like to talk Texas," he said. "That doesn't have to mean anything."

"You're not helping," Retta said quietly. "Tell me exactly how long it is since you last saw your mother."

"You know when that was. And I don't believe that I ever really *saw* her. I was only a baby, not more than a day or so old."

She nodded. "Nineteen years ago last June first, right? Somewhere in Waco, Texas. And how old was she then?"

"I told you all this back in Pennsylvania," he said, with some impatience."

"You said your mother was seventeen," she went on. "Seventeen and nineteen. That adds up to thirty-six. Isn't that about how old that blonde lady must be, the one selling broncos?"

"All right, all right," he said. "You're getting close, Retta. For a few minutes back there, I did think — not really *think*, but wonder — if my mother wouldn't be like that lady. The minute I saw her, I felt like I was remembering something."

"Tell me, Dallas."

"I don't think I can. I know I didn't really remember anything. I just got this sudden, odd feeling about her. It hit me in the heart so hard I thought my ribs had cracked."

She could see the deep inner trouble in his face. "But it wasn't true," he said. "I knew that almost right away. My birth mother would know me if she saw me. I look a lot like my father, except my eyes must be her color. I talked to the lady back there so she could hear my voice. I sound like my father."

"But why are you so concerned about how *I* reacted to the lady?"

"Because all this is about *us*," he said insistently. "This summer — well, just lately — we seem too far apart, too uneven. I know all about Retta Caldwell, where she lives, who she is. I know your family, where you work. You're *whole*, but I'm a guy made up of lots of pieces. I get the feeling you're not very curious about me. You don't seem to care where I'm coming from. I feel like I've got to prove something to you even if I don't know what."

"Am I supposed to understand what you're saying?" Retta asked with confusion.

He sighed. "What if that lady *had* been my mother? Do you know how important it is to me that my girl would *like* my mother? Or at least the kind of person my mother might be? It would help balance us out. I'm somebody, too, you know."

She put her hand on the steering wheel and was surprised to find it damp with the sweat of his palms.

"Let's turn around," Retta said. "We'll find that woman. We'll tell her your name. We'll ask her where she comes from. I'll even ask her right out, 'Ma'am, have you ever been in Waco, Texas?' "

He shook his head vigorously. "No! The whole thing was only my imagination. Just forget what I've been saying."

"I think we should turn around," Retta said again.

He slowed down a little and glanced at his wristwatch. "The rodeo will be over in about fifteen minutes. She'd be closed up. And besides, I've got these Arabians to think about."

He pressed hard on the gas and the tires screeched forward. "Why did you have to bring up an idea like that for, Retta? Like I said, it was my imagination. After tonight, I probably won't ever think of that lady again."

"All right, Dallas," she said. "But remember, *I* wanted to go back."

When they turned into the curved drive at the Bradleys', the van headlights picked out the yellow car parked just where she'd left it. From the barn, they could hear music on the radio and the soft tones of the Gomez brothers' lilting Spanish. Dallas jumped from the parked van and hurried to open the door on Retta's side.

They said neither good night nor good-bye. He touched her cheek with the back of his hand, then

140

kissed her lightly. "Let me call you," were his last words.

Moments later, as she slowed to make a right turn out of the driveway, Retta glanced in the rearview mirror. He was still standing where she'd left him, beside the horse van, looking after her car.

Chapter 11

It was a new experience for Retta to discover that a persistent silence can seem louder than actual noise. By late next evening, without a call from Rancho Arabian, the stillness of the telephone was like a pulsing, aching roar in her ears. On Thursday morning, she determined to spare herself the torment of waiting and wondering, and arranged to spend the entire day away from the house on Desert Lily.

First she went to the mall for two hours without buying anything, then ate a hot dog at a fast-food booth. When she dialed home, Two told her there had been no calls for her.

At the newspaper office, she decided to answer the half dozen letters readers had sent commenting on one of her columns. That took almost to the end of the working day. When she dialed home, Two's answer was still negative.

Mr. Caldwell came out of his office with a last-minute assignment: Go to City Hall with a tape recorder for the seven-thirty Council meeting, to record anything important for the weekly "Our Town" column the *Gazette* featured.

Two final items on the Council's agenda caused heated and lengthy debate. The meeting droned on till 10:30 in the evening.

When Retta arrived home, her parents were sitting outside at the pool. She heard her mother call out, the voice light and muffled through the closed door.

When Retta opened the sliding glass, her mother repeated the words. "Dallas called about an hour ago," she said. "I told him I'd let you know the moment you came in."

Though her parents were half shadowed by the citrus trees, Retta was aware of the bright moonlight, and the swimming pool shining both liquid and gilded. "Thanks. I'll call right away," she said.

"No, wait," her mother said. "He won't be there yet. He told me he planned to take one of the horses up on the desert for a workout."

"At *night?*" Retta said.

"Yes. He mentioned the moonlight. He plans to be back around midnight. I guess you could call him then."

"Did he say that? Call him at midnight?"

"No," Mrs. Caldwell said. "He didn't. He said nothing about calling him back. But I thought that's what he meant."

Retta showered, put on a cool nightgown, and lay

143

on her bed. Through the window, desert moonlight was silver-clear and a single palm tree from the front garden laid a fronded pattern across her bed.

She waited in the semidarkness till the hall clock chimed twelve, then went into the foyer to dial Dallas's quarters at Rancho Arabian. There was no answer.

A tiny, gnawing anxiety seemed to touch her heart. He must have known, Retta thought, that she would wait up to try to reach him at midnight. Or perhaps she'd reached a wrong number.

Suddenly a new idea struck her, a thought so persuasive that it managed to etch itself on her mind almost at once as a conviction. Things had been uneasy between them for some time, at least several days. He had said so himself on the drive down the mountains. *This summer — well, lately — we seem too far apart, too uneven.*

So he hadn't meant for her to get in touch with him at all. He himself had called earlier just to be polite. Dallas Dobson had decided to break up *his* way, little by little, to have their relationship over before he used that return ticket to Pennsylvania.

The silence of the last two days had been planned, carried out on purpose. He could be sitting in his quarters at this moment, hearing the sound of the phone, not caring, even wanting this chance to hurt her. He didn't need a Henrietta Caldwell in his life. His mind was made up. It was what he meant when he'd told her, "I'm somebody, too, you know."

She hesitated, then put the receiver back in place, not willing to risk a second call.

* * *

Two weeks earlier, when the family had made plans for a weekend in Los Angeles, Retta had decided not to go along, expecting to spend as much time as possible at Rancho Arabian. Now that departure time was near, she could not change her mind and make the trip. That would tell her family that things were no longer the same with Dallas, words she could not bear to say.

At seven o'clock on Friday evening, she stood in the driveway, shading her eyes against the desert sunset, and waved good-bye till the family car turned out of sight at the end of the street.

The day's mail lay in a wicker basket on a hall table. On top of the pile she saw a familiar green envelope addressed in the scrawled handwriting of Charlotte Amberson, Jr.

It had been more than three weeks since she'd heard from Charlotte, Retta realized, as she tore open the envelope. It was a long letter, three pages on both sides, sentences crammed together, words crossed out and written over.

"This isn't a subject I get a kick out of writing about, old friend," the first page began. *"But who can I tell? Truth is, Retta, we're broke and I'm getting scared. It's that bad.*

"We're going to get kicked out of this house, I'm sure. No rent payments made in months, almost since you left.

"One good thing: I'm ashamed of it and proud of him. Provanza (okay, my darling Sausage) has been smuggling bags of food out of the family store about twice a week. Mother pretends she doesn't know where the goodies come from, but she does.

"Mother also insists she's working on her novel, but — Henny Penny — typewriters make noise, don't they? I don't hear anything."

Retta folded the remaining pages without reading them and slipped the letter back into the envelope.

Forgive me, Charlie, she thought. I should start from the beginning and read to the end, then call you to talk about whatever can be done. But not now, Charlie. Some other time. I can't worry over your problems tonight. Not when I'm too confused to understand my own.

Retta made herself iced tea and took the frosted glass poolside. Alone in the still August heat, she sat thinking and brooding until long after nine o'clock, when the moon rose high enough to flood out the remote light of evening stars. The garden was touched everywhere with a melancholy lunar light, thin and eerie, more white than silver. Once this strange nightscape might have seemed precious, even sexually challenging to Retta, but now she was aware only of the personal loneliness of her surroundings, the significant silence of the phone.

Retreating to the house, she drew window shades and bolted the outside doors. For a few moments, near panic, she felt short of breath, almost faint. It was as if her fears, the reality of the breach with Dallas, were suffocating her.

The rest of the night Retta spent fully clothed, lying on her brother's bed, watching old movies on TV, the volume turned up just loud enough to drown out the hum of air-conditioning struggling against the sultry outdoor temperature.

Near morning, she was aware of experiencing a

146

series of fast, frightening dreams. They were not true nightmares, since she woke each time just before the huge, angry horses could reach the bed to trample her, but the great animals came so close that she could see their raw, sightless eyes and feel the ice of their breath.

When the alarm clock rang at seven in the morning, daylight was not welcome. Retta felt emotionally exhausted. There was a kind of shame in missing him so much, yet she was aware of a new sensation — a chill, growing resentment against the person who was the cause of this loneliness, the instigator of the dreams that shattered her night.

I can't let him make me helpless this way, she decided with weary finality. It all hurts too much. I'll stay out of this house all day. I won't know if he calls me or not.

Since the *Palms Gazette* published no Sunday edition, the office was empty on weekends except for Eddie Grant, a veteran reporter, touched now with arthritis, who answered phones and watched the wire services for breaking stories for Monday's paper. Mr. Grant sat at the computer switchboard, resting one swollen ankle on a bottoms-up wastebasket. He waved at Retta as she walked to a desk, then went back to his paperback novel.

During the morning, the switchboard lit up a few times and she could hear the murmur of Eddie Grant's voice and see his hunched shoulders as he made notes. She passed time by cleaning out the desk, then clipped and filed all the articles she had worked on in the past couple of months. At noontime, she drove to a fast-food outlet and brought back chicken tacos and root beer for both of them.

The big office stayed quiet most of the afternoon, the Saturday stillness broken only by the sound of the typewriter as Retta wrote and rewrote the Council meeting story, determined to make the task last through the day.

It was late afternoon when Eddie Grant called out her name. He signaled to the phone on her desk.

"Pick it up, Retta. Punch extension six."

"Is it my parents?"

"No," he said. "Some guy. I didn't ask for a name."

Retta picked up the phone. "Yes?" she said.

"Who is this?" the familiar voice asked.

"Who were you calling?" she said, feeling the sudden, quickened beat of her heart.

"Oh, come on," Dallas said with impatience. "Is this Henrietta Caldwell, or isn't it?"

"Of course, it's Henrietta," she answered, willing her voice to stay controlled. "What made you think I'd be *here?* I never come in on Saturdays."

"You certainly weren't at home," he said. "No one is. I've called there a dozen times in the last couple of hours. You might have let me know where to reach you, Retta."

"I tried to reach *you* Thursday night."

There was a small silence. "Well, I'm sorry about that," he said finally. "I was in the high desert working with Arista. It took longer than I thought."

"I called at exactly midnight," she said. "Were you there, Dallas?"

"Of course not," he said with surprise. "If I was, I would have answered."

"I just wasn't sure about that."

"Believe me, Retta, I didn't get Arista into her stall

148

until almost two o'clock. It was too late then to call you."

She checked herself against mentioning the silence of yesterday, the long hours of last night. Again there was a pause at the other end of the line.

"What I'm calling about now, Retta," he said at last, "is about tonight. I wanted to be sure you could keep our date."

"I didn't know we had a date, Dallas."

She heard the sharp intake of breath. "What is this, Retta? What are you saying? I thought we always tried to be together on Saturday night."

"Even this Saturday?" she asked, almost afraid of his answer.

"*Especially* this Saturday," he said. "There's so little time left. I've been counting on it. I need to see you out here at Rancho Arabian."

"Why there?" She felt a stir of uneasiness, puzzled by the unspoken urgency of his request. "I'm not sure I want to come out there."

"Don't be that way," he said. "Please. You may think you have a reason to be mad at me, but you haven't. Not any *real* reason." He was talking loudly now. "This is so important to me, Retta. I've never asked you for a special favor before, have I?"

"Has something happened to you?" she asked. "There's something wrong, isn't there? Is it about the Bradleys? Or is it your father, Dallas?"

"Because I want to see my girl, does something have to be *wrong?*" he said. "I want you to come to the ranch, that's all. I want you here at six-thirty."

"Well," she said, trying to come to a decision, "I have some work to finish here. Maybe I could be there by seven-thirty."

149

"You don't seem to hear me right. I can't count on the Gomez brothers tonight; Eddie drove to Tijuana to pick up his grandmother. And Chico cut his hand on bailing wire this afternoon. He called me from the clinic. He's got thirteen stitches."

"But I'd need to shower and change . . ."

"Please, Retta. Do this for me. Don't make me explain," he said.

The strain in his voice, the dark tone of his words, troubled her. "Listen, Dallas," she said quickly. "I don't really have to do those things I said. I'll drive out right now."

"No," he answered. "Come at six-thirty, quarter to seven at the latest. I'm not ready for you now. Don't let me down, Retta."

He hung up quickly, before she had a chance to answer, and before she had time to change her mind.

Chapter
12

When Henrietta turned in the gate at six-thirty, the Bradley property had a quiet, near-deserted look about it. The family had flown to Scottsdale a few days earlier, and the redwood doors of the big garage were shut. In the ranch house itself, all the white window draperies had been closed, giving the structure an oddly human appearance, a shut-eyed quality like something caught unexpectedly asleep.

Retta paused beside the exercise ring, puzzled by the silence and lack of ranch activity. She shaded her eyes against the late afternoon glare to look around, trying to search out movement anywhere, but there was no one in sight.

The entire scene—from the sandy exercise ring

and barnyard, then stretching out past the silhou-
etted horses in the corrals and onto the distant rim
of the mountains—was touched with the light pink-
gold of an August sunset. Dallas Dobson was nowhere in sight.

Retta called out his name, then waited. She
walked to the bunkhouse and tapped lightly on the
window, peering through the dusty pane. When no
one answered, she hurried to the main barn, calling
his name again. She tried to open the slide rod that
held the door shut, but the bolt was stiff in her hand.
The resistance told her someone had locked the
heavy door from the inside.

It was then she first noticed the horse van, at one
side of the barn, pulled into an alcove of shadow.
The vehicle had been freshly washed and waxed,
red and gray ribbons were looped and festooned
from the radiator ornament. Whitewall tires had
been scrubbed clean, and even the hubcaps flashed
in the sunlight, as bright and buffed as precious
metal.

She turned to the barn door again, pounding it
with both hands, calling out Dallas's name. From
inside, a voice answered, muffled and impatient.
She could not make out who was speaking or what
had been said.

Retta stood perfectly still, the sun beating hot
against her back, and listened to the shuffle of movement behind the door. She glanced at her wristwatch. Nearly five minutes passed before she could
hear the distinctive sound of stacked heels approaching and the *plod-plod* of a single horse being
led along the cemented passageway.

Interior locks turned, the doors swung inward.

Dallas stepped out, blinking in the brilliant sunlight, leading the horse, Arista, by the bridle.

"Sorry to keep you waiting," he said immediately. "I wanted the hoof wax to dry hard before taking Arista out into the dust and sand."

"Hoof wax?" she heard herself echo.

He pointed to the horse's four hooves, shining as smoothly lustrous as brown, silken leather. "I mixed dark shoe polish in with the wax," he said. "It accents the hoof and brings out Arista's silver coloring. See how slim the leg looks above the fetlock?"

She listened but seemed to find no meaning in his words. For the moment, it was Dallas himself who held Retta's attention. He seemed taller than she had ever noticed, standing in his boots with the star of Texas on each ankle, worn leather and stacked heels burnished with care.

He was wearing a denim shirt, carefully pressed, and Levis so skintight that she suspected he had used the old "shrink trick" of pouring hot water on the jeans when he was already wearing them. Body heat had dried the fabric so it fitted like a second skin over his lean hips and muscled legs. As he moved closer, she caught the scent of talcum powder, lemon shampoo, and a touch of saddle soap.

"Is this too much?" he asked, touching a band of twisted blue denim knotted as a sweatband around his forehead. "I tore it off the tail of the shirt. I think Arista will stand out more if I'm in the background, wearing simple clothes, all one color. What do you think, Retta? Does the headband look okay?"

He stepped directly in front of her, shoulders erect, face impassive, waiting for an answer. Once again, she felt she might be looking at a stranger, someone too aggressively handsome and mature to be the reserved almost shy person she knew back in Pennsylvania.

Dobson had not had a haircut all summer and his long, dark hair was twisted at the nape of his neck, tied with a scrap of denim. Weeks of summer sun laid a dark polish on his cheekbones, accenting his gray-green eyes.

He seemed calm, almost at ease, but Henrietta noticed that his face and chest, at the open shirt, were shining with perspiration and tiny beads of sweat glistened on the tips of his eyelashes.

At that moment, Arista shook her great head and the ornate silver discs that hung from the tooled leather headband arching under the forelock, ear to ear, sang out like the tinkle of tiny bells.

Retta stared, fascinated, trying to absorb every detail of the horse's elaborate gear, yet she was unable to comprehend the meaning of this unexpected display. This was not the familiar Arista, the classic, pure Arabian, the unadorned, natural prize of the whole ranch. Now the great horse was caparisoned in fancy leather, expensive, ornate silver trappings and decorations, and shiny red and gray ribbons. She stood bedecked and restless in the late August sunlight like some strange, equine bride.

Retta felt her mouth go dry and her stomach muscles tighten with fear. She knew exactly, and with deep apprehension, just where this priceless finery had come from.

Arista whinnied and shook her head again, aware of all the strange ornaments decorating her muscled body. Retta reached out to touch one of the dozen or more heavy silver discs that hung from the embossed leather saddle, and the metal was surprisingly cold to her touch.

"Dallas," she whispered, as if someone somewhere on the vast, silent ranch might overhear, "you opened the Bradleys' locked vault in the lab room. These are their *treasures*, the things you wouldn't even let me *see*. The silver things, all those other trappings — they must be worth thousands of dollars."

"The Bradleys gave me that key," he said defiantly. "They know I have it."

"But they gave it to you for safekeeping, for an emergency. Not to *use*."

"This *is* an emergency," he said. "I *need* Arista tonight. I *need* this fancy gear."

"What is it, Dallas? I don't hear from you for nearly three days, and now *this*. You've got to tell me." He reached out to take her hand, but she drew away from him. "It's like you're stealing," she said in a hushed voice.

"I'm only *borrowing* the horses and this expensive stuff," he said harshly. "And I'll only be *gone* a few hours. . . ."

"You mean we're going somewhere with Arista?"

"Not *us*, Retta. *I'm* going somewhere. I'm going up to Danning to the rodeo. Fargo Haynes came up with a big idea for the last night. He wants to show people he's still a star." His voice rose with a surge of enthusiasm.

"It's like I've been waiting all my life for this," he said. "The other night, when I went back to Haynes's trailer, he told me his idea. It's been talked up all over country radio for the last couple of days. We'll get a big crowd."

"I haven't been listening to country radio," she said.

"They're calling it the Fargo Haynes Riding Championship. It's a competition for the best horses and fancy riders. Haynes is putting up the prize money and trophy. I've been practicing with Arista every day; nights, too. I'll use everything this horse knows and everything my brother taught me. A couple of stunt riders are coming down from Hollywood. And an Indian fellow — Star Dog, he's called — will be over from the reservation. The man used to be good, Haynes says, but he's old now, with a nag for a horse.

"I'm the fourth contestant. I've got to win fair and square, no doubt about that, but Fargo Haynes is the only judge, and I know he respects me after the other night. And no horse will look better than Arista."

"Were you going to tell me about this, Dallas?"

He shrugged. "I planned to drive over to your house first thing in the morning, when one of the Gomezes showed up here. I'd have the prize money to show you — a check for five hundred dollars — and more important, a silver belt buckle right out of Fargo Haynes's personal wardrobe. That's the winner's trophy, a cowboy buckle with ruby chips and Haynes's initials in the middle. The winner's name will be engraved on the back."

"Let's talk about me now," Retta said quietly. "How do I fit into this plan?"

Dallas began to pace, taking short, brisk steps, and to rub his hands together vigorously, as if they were cold.

"The Bradleys will be in Arizona at least until

156

Monday," he said. "I told you on the phone what happened to the Gomez brothers. Well, I've got everything here in perfect order — the feeding, the watering, the cleanup. All I need is for you to baby-sit the place for me."

"I know almost nothing about horses," Retta protested. "And this is a big place. . . ."

"I'll be back in three hours, long before midnight," he said impatiently.

When she shook her head, he stared at her in disbelief. "But I'm doing this for *both of us*." His voice was loud, urgent. "Can't you understand that, Retta?"

"No, I can't. Not when you're talking crazy this way. You tell me you're leaving Rancho Arabian unattended. You're taking the Bradleys' best horse without permission. You're risking thousands of dollars of heirlooms . . . how can you say you're doing this for *us?*"

He put a hand on each side of her face, forcing her to look at him. "There's more to this than I told you," he said. "It wasn't a promise exactly, but in his trailer, Haynes hinted that if I win tonight, he might be able to use me in Hollywood. I could work his horses, maybe ride sidekick when he makes public appearances. With luck, I could get to be his stuntman, his double in movies."

"Is that what you want?" Retta asked.

"That's what I want," he said, his voice firm. "Then I won't *have* to take that scholarship. I won't *have* to go back to Pennsylvania. We can be together, Retta. I can see you almost every weekend. You wouldn't need to bother with other guys. Not if I have a job right here in California."

157

"You've got a job right here and right now," Retta protested. "You're responsible for every building, every animal on this property. The Bradleys pay you to keep your word, and they trust you. Isn't that more important than any secondhand belt buckle?"

"No," he said stubbornly. "This is the big chance, and guys like me don't always *get* the big chance. That buckle is going to have my name on it. I can send it to my father, tell him I won the first prize right from Fargo Haynes himself."

"Your father!" Retta said. "You're taking the chance of being fired, maybe getting arrested and going to prison — you're risking your whole future just to show off for your *father?*"

When he put his hand on her shoulder, she could feel the trembling. "My father's not an easy man. You know that, Retta. I haven't heard from him once since I left."

"And that buckle could make a difference?"

He tightened his grip. "Yes. I need to show him I can be a winner. You never saw my father's face when Sam Houston came home with trophies. I *have* to go to Danning tonight."

"Don't pretend you *have to*, Dallas. And you're not doing this for *us*. Don't pretend that, either."

Dallas's face went tight with anger and he slapped a fist into his open palm so hard that it sounded like a pistol shot. Arista whinnied softly and laid back her ears in alarm. Automatically, Dallas reached out to the big horse and put a soothing hand on her cheek.

Then he said to Retta, "If you won't let me win for us, then I'll win for myself. You're not going to stop me."

158

"Go, then," she said. "You've made up your mind. But what do you expect to do if the Bradleys find out?"

He looked at her with narrowed eyes. "Does that mean you plan to *tell* them?"

"No, I don't plan to tell them," she said evenly. "After tonight I don't expect to be at Rancho Arabian ever again."

The finality of her own words filled her with a deep sadness. She remembered, with a start of guilt, that just a few nights before it was she who had goaded him, urged him to make decisions for himself. Now he had done just that.

She glanced at her watch. "It's after seven. You're going to be late."

He looked at her for several moments in silence. When he spoke again, his voice was calm, almost normal. "I'll turn the outside lights on for you," he said. "For later, when it starts getting dark."

As he walked to the electrical-panel box mounted on the wall outside his quarters, Retta followed him. He pulled switch after switch, turning on lights at both ends of the barn, in the feed lot area, at the birthing shed, in the corrals, and on out to the farthest reaches of the fence lines. The familiar symmetries of the ranch buildings and split-rail boundaries stood out stark and clear.

"And here's the monitor dial for the TV equipment covering the stables," Dallas explained, pointing to a numbered plastic indicator. Then he gestured toward a small TV screen above the door. "Turn on the system, adjust the dial, and you can get sight and sound from any area in the stable. There's a second screen in the Bradleys' bedroom for when they're home."

"You showed me all this gear last June, the first day," she said. "I won't use it. As soon as you get the horse van out of here, I'll pull my own car over by those palm trees and sit in it till you get back."

"At least you should know how all this works," he said. "For the past couple of weeks we've focused mostly on Estrella." He turned the dial to "ON" and "STALL 8" and a close-up of Estrella showed clearly on the TV screen above the door, the big, pregnant mare panting and staring head-on into the lens.

"Just turn that thing off and *go*, Dallas," she said insistently. "Go to Danning and get this over with!"

He hesitated, then touched her hand. His fingers were light but hot, with a burning texture as if he had a fever. "Can't you wish me luck, Henrietta?"

"Yes. I wish you luck, Dallas. Now take Arista — "

At that moment, they were both aware of a neighing sound, a quick, equine cry of distress. They turned at once to Arista, still tethered at the barn, but that mare was standing quietly, a silver horse decked with silver ornaments, luminous under the intense beams of the yard lights.

In unison, they turned to look at the TV screen above the door and Dallas cried out aloud at what he saw.

"No, no, not Estrella! Not tonight." His voice was an anguished shout. "I've got to get to Danning. I've *got* to. No way I'll pass up this chance. . . ."

The bay mare, the barrel of her body taut and rounded, was now standing side-view to the camera focused on her stall. She whinnied wildly again, tossing her mane. Then she pawed sharply with her front hooves and minced backward a few short steps, lashing her raised tail.

160

A radical change was passing over the horse's entire body. Dallas and Retta watched in stunned silence as the great mare became aware of her own condition. Estrella craned her neck to look backward over her torso, seeming to observe the new, involuntary movements, the sudden pattern of rhythmic spasms moving backward, from chest to hindquarters, rippling and stretching the tight, ballooning horsehide.

"Is she sick?" Retta asked. "Is that what's wrong with her?"

Suddenly, Estrella lifted the heavy brush of her tail higher and a gush of murky liquid spilled to the straw scattered on the floor.

"This can't be," Dallas said, as if talking to himself. "The bag of water just broke. But Dr. Meacham was here three nights ago. He said she was fine, right on schedule."

He pulled the strip of denim off his forehead and began winding it round and round his hand as he paced.

"I reread her charts in the lab just this morning. She was bred last October twentieth. Give or take a few days, she wasn't due till the middle of next month. The Bradleys planned to be here. This isn't even my responsibility. . . ."

Now the horse was emitting a series of loud grunts, and with front legs bending at the knee joints, she lowered herself cautiously onto the straw, then rolled awkwardly onto one side, pulling and straining.

"She seems to be retching," Retta said.

"She's in labor," Dallas replied. "Premature maybe, but she's ready to foal. I've got to get her into the birthing shed till we can get some help. She could crush a newborn in that narrow stall."

As he started for the barn, he shouted, "Get Dr. Meacham, Retta. His number is by the phone in my room. If he comes right away, I could still have that chance. . . ."

She found a list of phone numbers pinned to the wall inside the bunkhouse and dialed the office of Dr. Reynolds Meacham, veterinarian, in Indio. After four rings, she was connected to a tape recorder that gave instructions to leave name and phone number, the doctor would call back on Monday.

Frantically, she leafed through the local phone book until she found a number for the Meachams' home. As the phone rang again and again somewhere out in Indio, she glanced around the small, spare room.

There was a neatly made bed, some worn bedroom furniture, and a small hot plate on the windowsill. On a nightstand next to the bed were two framed color snapshots. The first was familiar. It was a picture taken of the two of them at last year's Havendale High prom.

The second picture was a shot of a young man she had never seen before, but recognized at once. He was standing next to a pinto horse, an almost exact likeness of his younger brother, but blue-eyed and fair-haired. The blue tones of the denim jeans and Texas sky in the picture had begun to fade, but the eyes were still vivid. Next to the two pictures stood the little windup bronco toy.

At that moment, Mrs. Meacham in Indio answered the phone. She explained the situation quickly. There was never anyone in the office on Saturday night. Her husband's assistant, Dr. Towne, was in Los Angeles at the International Biped Conference. Dr. Meacham himself was the attending veterinarian at the rodeo grounds in Danning tonight at the request of an old friend, Fargo Haynes. No, the doctor had left no phone number at which he could be reached.

Leafing through the Yellow Pages, Retta found nothing listed under "Rodeo" or "Fairgrounds." In the silent room, the loud ticking of an alarm clock drew her attention. More than ten minutes had passed since she came to call for help.

Frantic, she dialed Information. An operator put the question to her computer and determined quickly that there was no permanent listing for a phone at the rodeo or fairgrounds in Danning. During September each year, there were special hookups installed for the County Fair. At this time, however, there was no active phone connection.

Chapter
13

Retta had never been in the white, one-story birthing shed before. Her fingers trembled as she turned the doorknob.

Inside was a large room, each corner contoured and rounded so the floor area was a soft-edged rectangle without sharp, confining angles. A cooling unit hummed from the ceiling, sending currents of air down to rustle over the thick layer of peanut shells that covered the cement floor. Muted rays shone from frosted neon bars that laced the ceiling, light easy on the eyes, but illuminating everything with pinpoint clarity.

A zinc-topped table was arranged with scissors, instruments, rolls of bandages, iodine, alcohol, and several pairs of rubber gloves. An electric stove nearby held a large white porcelain cooker, boiling water already sending steam out from under the heavy lid.

Estrella stood in the middle of the birthing room, eyes bright, with wild, short grunts escaping from her throat as labor contractions came and went. The flowing tail had been bound tight with clean, heavy bandages and bundled up high, above and away from the body.

Dallas still wore his denim shirt and tight jeans but he had removed his boots and socks. Rubber surgical gloves covered both hands and the dry peanut husks cracked and rustled under his bare feet.

With a sponge and a steaming bucket of milky liquid that smelled strongly of disinfectant, he was bathing the horse's flanks and hind quarters.

"I've got to get her sterilized before she wants to lie down again," he said. "I've been trying to time the contractions but they don't seem regular yet. Or else I'm missing some. When can Meacham get here?"

"I couldn't reach him" Retta said quickly. "And his assistant is in Los Angeles. Dr. Meacham is at the rodeo tonight. The only other vets listed in the phone book are way up in Riverside. Even if I could reach them, that's more than three hours away."

Dallas stood motionless, staring at her, the sponge dripping liquid down his legs. In spite of the cool air blowing into the room, his face was shining with sweat.

"You didn't *talk* to Meacham?" he said in a stunned voice. "You can't get me *anyone?*" He bent over suddenly, hugging his chest with both arms and rocking from side to side. "This can't be happening," he said. "I have my *own* plans for tonight. Why does Estrella have to depend on *me?*"

"Are you hurt, Dallas? Are you in pain somewhere?" Retta asked anxiously.

He stood up then and his eyes looked dark with shock. "Yes, I'm in pain," he said. "I'm *scared*, Retta. I don't *know* enough about foaling. I can exercise, feed, and clean up, even shoe a horse if I have to, but birthing . . ." He shook his head in disbelief.

"Can't you just sort of . . . help?" Retta asked.

"Help! What can I do? I read all the books in the barn library. I studied the pictures, but this is real. I've never *helped*, I've never even *watched* before. What if the foal is in the wrong position? What if there is hemorrhaging? What if I do something wrong?"

"How much time do we have?" Retta asked.

Dallas frowned, then shrugged. "I just don't know. It's a first foal for Estrella. It could be up to eight hours, even longer. Or it could be a quick one, two hours, or less."

"What do you want me to do, Dallas?" she asked helplessly.

He was silent for a long moment, lost in his own thoughts. Then he came to a decision. Ripping his shirt off over his head, without unbuttoning it, he tossed it into a corner. With a surgical knife from the zinc-topped table, he sliced open the legs of his tight jeans and rolled the cloth tight above his knees.

"There's only one way we can do this," he said. "I stay with Estrella. I try to remember everything I know, help out any way that seems right. Do the best I can."

He put a hand on Retta's shoulder and she could feel the trembling. "You drive up fast to Danning, but be careful. Find Dr. Meacham, get him down here. Can you do that for me, Retta?"

She nodded. "It should be forty minutes up, forty minutes back," she said, her hand already on the doorknob. "Maybe less."

"*Careful*," he repeated. "It's Saturday night. Could be extra traffic or mountain fog up there."

But those were not his last words. As she stepped out into the warm, heavy desert air, he called after her. "And, Retta, if you see Fargo Haynes — let him know I planned to win tonight."

For the first few miles, she stayed in the right-hand lane at a medium speed, aware of the white stone markers at the side of the road that indicated drops into sandy ditches and, farther on toward the mountains, deep, rocky ravines.

In the foothills, traffic was fast and heavy, but gradually those cars sped past her and disappeared into the darkness leading to Danning. As the vehicles around her thinned, Retta pressed her foot on the accelerator, feeling the sturdy chassis of the small car shiver as the speed moved up to a legal 55 miles per hour.

She'd had her driver's license for nearly a year, but this was the first time she had taken her car out alone on a major high-speed highway at night.

Several miles from Danning, the electric glow from the fairground lights began to beam illumination into the black sky. Some minutes later, when the speed gauge rose to an alarming 65 miles per hour, she lightened her foot on the gas pedal and breathed deeply several times to relieve the tension crowding her heart.

As Dallas predicted, attendance at the rodeo was heavy. A sprawl of parked cars extended right out to the main gate. Retta pulled close to a road bank just outside the entrance, ready for a fast departure once she had done what she meant to do.

Hurrying up the rutted lane, she made a sharp right to where she hoped Fargo Haynes's trailer was still parked. It was there, but dark and locked now.

In a stumbling run, she sped toward the lights and music some distance away, breath catching short, finally breaking through the crowd of spectators near the entrance to the main ring.

Fargo Haynes was there as she had so desperately hoped, leaning on a fence, overhead lights shining on his white buckskins and Stetson hat. Tonight he was wearing show business makeup — deep-tan face coloring, with reddened cheeks and a touch of silver brushed over his thick eyebrows and full mustache.

On one side of Haynes stood a tall, muscular man in jeans and a red shirt with an armband reading "Official." On the other side was a short, wiry male of about fifty, lean and brown-skinned, showing the sharp, high features of a Norongo Indian.

At that moment, Haynes caught sight of Retta and swept off his hat in greeting. "Hello there, young lady," he said. "We're waiting for your boyfriend to put some class into this show."

168

"Oh, please," she said quickly. "Dallas is at the ranch. He's not coming here tonight. I've got to find Dr. Meacham. I promised to find him."

The man in the red shirt turned sharply. "I'm Meacham," he said.

In her relief, words came tumbling out, making little sense to Retta, but Dr. Meacham listened attentively and had already begun to unpin the band from his shirt sleeve.

He handed the armband to the Norongan, then said to Haynes, "Estrella is on my charts for mid-September. I'd never have come up here tonight if I'd known that mare was ready."

Then he spoke directly to Retta. "I'll take my own car. I know some back roads. That's a damned valuable animal down there."

He turned and pushed his way quickly through the crowd.

"I'll escort you back to your vehicle, miss," Fargo Haynes said formally, holding his big white hat against his chest.

"No, no, thank you," she said. "I must hurry. I'll have to run all the way. But I have an important message to give you. Dallas said to tell you he had planned to win tonight. . . ."

Haynes looked thoughtful, then said, "I hope you appreciate, little lady, that you've got yourself a very special cowboy."

Retta felt an unwanted touch of resentment at the old man's patronizing tone. "I haven't 'got' anyone, Mr. Haynes," she said. "Dallas Dobson is his own man."

Haynes laughed and laid a big hand lightly on

her shoulder. "Exactly, little lady," he said. "That's just what I meant."

From the moment she'd turned the car out of Rancho Arabian, Retta knew there were three people she wanted to find at the rodeo that night. Dr. Reynolds Meacham and Fargo Haynes were the first two. She prayed now that she was not too late to find the last.

Her mouth went dry with tension as she headed away from the show ring and up to the narrow strip of midway where the food stands and souvenir booths were located.

"Please," she begged some unnamed fate, *"please let her still be there."*

"I sure hope your brother likes it," the woman said in her soft Texas drawl when Retta selected the bronco she wanted. "I'm sorry I can't wrap it, but I got nothing but these little brown bags."

"Don't worry," Retta said as she held out a five-dollar bill. "I have birthday paper at home I can use."

The woman dug into her pockets for change. From under her white cowgirl hat, blue eyes were watching Retta quizzically.

"Weren't you here a few nights ago, near closing time, with a tall, good-looking fellow?" she asked.

Retta felt her heart pulse faster. "Yes, I was," she said. "Thursday night. How come you remember? Did you know that fellow?"

The woman was thoughtful. "I don't think so," she said. "In fact, I'm sure not."

170

"Well, did he remind you of someone?"

"Not that, either," the lady answered. "But I'd remember him next time. He sure is good-looking, and nice, too. He your boyfriend?"

"Yes," Retta said. She tried to moisten her lips, now almost too stiff to form the necessary words. "His father is Daniel Dobson; Danny Dobson, some people call him. My boyfriend's name is Dallas."

"The only Daniel I know is in the Bible," the woman said. "Dallas? That's a good name for a cowboy. He come from that town?"

"No," Retta said. "Dallas Dobson was born in Waco, Texas. He turned nineteen this June first." When the woman did not respond, Retta said, "Do you know Waco, Texas, ma'am?"

The lady smiled and shook her head so the stubby blonde pigtails swung against her cheeks. "I'm a small-town girl. I don't know any of them big places like Houston or El Paso or Waco. My folks all come from Ozone in Crockett County, only about three thousand people. That's in the Panhandle. Now I move around a lot. I married a guy who works these rodeos."

"And you don't get tired of moving around? With the baby coming and all?"

The lady handed Retta her change. "Don't let anyone scare you, honey," she said softly. "Having a baby isn't all that hard. Of course, I'm a little old for the first one."

"You never had a child before?" Retta asked, watching the woman's face so closely she knew she would remember that direct gaze, the shy smile as long as she lived.

"This is my first," the woman said. Under the heavy makeup, her cheeks went pink and there was a look of tears in her eyes. "Some people say I'm crazy to have a first child at my age. But we want this baby, my husband and I, no matter what."

Retta was suddenly aware that she had been holding the plastic bronco so tightly that the hooves were biting painfully into the palm of her hand. Yet the sharp physical discomfort seemed to loosen the emotional tensions. She relaxed her hand.

"I'm glad I talked to you," she said. "I hope you have a wonderful baby."

"What's your name, honey?" the lady asked. "We still can't decide on what to call it if it's a girl."

"Henrietta," Retta said.

The woman's tone became apologetic. "That's a nice name, just right for *you*. But it's kind of old-fashioned. What do you think of Bluebonnet? That's the Texas state flower, you know."

"It's a lovely name," Retta said as she turned to leave. "She'd probably be called Bonnie most of the time."

"I'd like that," the woman said, her face brightening. "You're a nice person, just like your boyfriend. Be sure to say hello to him for me. I'm sorry he and I never got to talk about Texas."

Retta nodded, glancing at her wristwatch. She left the midway at a fast walk, then broke into a run. Nearly twelve minutes had passed since Dr. Meacham left the show ring to drive to Rancho Arabian.

All the way down the long, rutted road, until she reached the yellow car parked outside the gates, the precious words she could now say kept running through her mind like an insistent mantra: Dallas, Dallas! You didn't lose your mother *twice*. That blonde lady has never even been in Waco. . . .

When she reached the ranch at last, the scene was not as she'd left it. Most of the outside lights had been switched off. Dr. Meacham's car was parked askew on the driveway, engine turned off but the headlights on, as if he had just swerved to a stop and jumped out quickly.

The car lights shone on Estrella, standing in the corral outside the birthing shed, a small, teetering creature beside her. Retta caught her breath at the sight of this mauve-gray foal, swaying on thin legs, knobbed and rickety as bamboo poles. The newly born animal leaned against the mare's flank, still weak but already nuzzling and nursing.

As she walked toward the scene, Retta felt an unexpected softness in her knees. She paused to lean on the split-rail fencing, almost faint with an enervating feeling of relief and joy.

Dr. Meacham knelt at one side of the corral, looking through his medical bag, conversing with Dallas in a low voice. Dallas was talking to the doctor in short, rapid bursts, gesturing as he spoke. A long yellow tape measure hung around his neck.

The doctor moved to the mare's side, listened repeatedly with his stethoscope, then began to run experienced hands over the still-swollen body.

"I've got both animals cleaned up pretty good, Doctor. You can see that," Dallas said. Dr. Meacham nodded in approval.

"The membranes over the head and nose broke naturally, like it should, I guess. I cleared out the nostrils with swabbing," Dallas continued.

"It looks like a clean birth," the doctor said quietly.

Dallas was standing close, watching the veterinarian's moves intently. "Like the books say, when Estrella completed labor and was calm, I gave her a bran feed. Then I tried to get the filly on her feet. It took no more than ten or fifteen minutes till she was standing by herself."

"You did just right, Dallas," Dr. Meacham said. "Giving birth is a hard business."

The vet was down on his knees now, examining the newborn foal, passing an expert hand over the head, eyes, and ears, and then the entire small, trembling body, searching for any irregularity or deformity. Estrella moved closer and nudged against the doctor's hand with her nose. "Okay, lady," the doctor said soothingly. "We're both on the same team here."

Then, in silence, the man spent some time inspecting the big mare before he spoke again. "Good. We don't have to worry about infection and fever, or blood poisoning, either."

Dallas touched the measuring tape still hanging around his neck. "I tape-weighed the little one," he said. "I'm inexperienced at it, but I think she weighs about fifty pounds."

"I expect you're about right. A good job all round." The doctor put a hand on Dallas's shoulder. "Congratulations to all three of you. I'll stop by around seven tomorrow morning to check things out."

"Something I forgot to mention," Dallas said. "I called the Bradleys in Scottsdale just before you got here. All three took turns on the line, they were so excited. They'd like you to call them, too."

"I'm going directly home now. I'll call them from there. You can be proud of the job you did, Dallas."

"Can you tell me something, Doctor?" Dallas asked. "What are the rules about naming a foal? You'll notice this one has a white marking below the forehead, just like her mother. I'd like to call her Little Star. Can I do that?"

Meacham shook his head. "That decision is up to the owners. The Bradleys will want to pick a name that fits with ancestors and bloodlines, that sort of thing."

"All right, but until the Bradleys get home, we're going to call this baby Little Star. No, make that Estrellita," Dallas said.

Twice, while Dallas and Dr. Meacham were talking, Retta heard heavy movement, then metallic, bell-like sounds. She became aware of Arista, tethered in shadows at the far side of the bar, still wearing the elaborate leather and silver trappings.

When Dr. Meacham's car pulled out the gate, taillights winking like fireflies into the darkness, Retta spoke aloud for the first time since leaving the rodeo grounds.

"Dallas," she said, "let me help you. Let's get those valuable things off Arista and back into the vault."

"No," he answered quietly. "I took them out. I'll put them back. Just wait here for me, Retta."

He unhitched the decorated mare and led her into the stables. Retta climbed the corral fencing and walked slowly toward Estrella. She put a hand on the big horse's muzzle and whispered some soothing words before kneeling down to look at Estrellita.

The young horse was skittish at the nearness of a stranger. It trembled under the touch of Retta's fingers as she felt the knobby legs, the velvet nose, and the delicate ridge of spine.

Retta pressed her face gently against the soft white star under the forelock. "It's like a miracle, Estrellita. As if . . . as if *we* had a baby tonight."

Looking at the fresh perfection of the infant animal, awed by the reality of new life, Retta became aware of her own tired body, dusty hair, and damp, wrinkled clothing. She remembered the outdoor faucet located over the mint bed at one side of the bar.

The first liquid out of the faucet felt warm as she splashed it over her weary face and closed eyes. When the water came out more fresh, she bent low to drink directly from the spout, working the coolness around and around in her mouth before letting it trickle down her throat. Up from the ground beneath her feet rose the sharp scent of trampled mint.

Feeling protected in the semidarkness, she plucked some of the coarse leaves and chewed them slowly, sucking the bitter spearmint until her mouth, teeth, and tongue were fresh, and the strong saliva burned sharp and nipping against her lips.

She slipped off her sneakers and socks to feel the matted green leaves cool and refreshing under her bare feet. Impulsively, she pulled the damp T-shirt off over her head and bent to tear up bunches of the tough, scented herb until both hands were filled.

Standing in the shadows, the outlines of her body barely touched by the lights in the corral, she rubbed the pungent mint on her tired legs and thighs, then stroked it vigorously over her bare shoulders, back, and breasts. Tearing up fresh handfuls, she brushed the leaves over her hair and under the damp curls at her neck.

In moments, her tired body felt bathed and renewed by the rough texture and strong fragrance of the aromatic plants. All her senses came acutely awake, challenged and stirred by the sting of peppery juices over her warm, bare skin. It was an experience of wonder and joy.

I can't understand just what happened tonight, she thought dreamily, but it has happened for both of us, I'm sure of that.

Lost in her own reflections, Retta stood motionless, eyes half closed, facing out toward the far rim of the mountains, barely aware of a small night breeze as it moved to dry the mint juices on her skin.

Then she heard Dallas, over at the corral, calling out her name. "I'm here," she whispered as she picked up the T-shirt and pulled it quickly over her head.

To Retta, it seemed as if they were isolated together in the windless core of this black and blessed evening, a night that whispered with oleander bushes, the sleepy movements of horses in the barn, and the nearby, contented snuffling of the nursing foal. She was acutely aware of mint fragrance, the drift of sandalwood scent from the open desert, and the heat of Dallas's bare arms and chest, all mingled with the deeply stirring odors of new birth still clinging to his big hands.

As she had come toward him from the shadows, he held out both arms to embrace her. She could feel the warmth of his words spoken softly against her damp hair.

"When I first saw the foal, when I knew for sure it was going to live and breathe, I wanted to sing or cry or shoot a gun into the sky. I wanted *noise*. So I shouted, 'Look, Retta, look!' Did you hear me?" He looked down at her.

"No," she whispered, her face tight against his chest.

He laughed. "Maybe I wasn't as loud as I thought I was. But all of a sudden everything seemed clear. I didn't even have to think about it."

He put a finger under her chin and lifted her face. He kissed her then, lightly, barely touching her lips, as if his mind were on something else.

"I'm going back to Pennsylvania on schedule, Retta," he said. "I suppose you've guessed that. I can do it now. I'll take that scholarship, work my way through. And handle my father no matter what it takes. And most important, it's going to be all right with us. After tonight, I believe that."

"I can almost promise you, Dallas." She moved out of his arms and stepped back to look up at him. "There's something else you should know. Something you need to know. . . ."

She paused. "I did something tonight before I drove back from Danning. I found that blonde woman again, the one with the broncos. I talked with her. I asked her questions, lots of questions. She's a nice person, just as you thought, and she *is* from Texas. But she's not your mother."

Carefully remembering every word, every facial expression, she told him what she had said to the woman in the white cowgirl outfit, and what the woman had said to her. He studied her intently, standing so still that he almost seemed to have stopped breathing.

"She's never had a baby before, Dallas," she said finally. "And she's never even *been* to Waco."

When he spoke, his words surprised her. His only comment, only question was, "Retta, you did this for *me?*"

She felt the sting of tears in her eyes. "For both of us. I wanted to be sure nothing was my fault, that you hadn't lost your mother again because we weren't getting along, or because of something I said. But you didn't lose her, Dallas. You just haven't *found* her yet."

He held her in one arm, smoothing her tangled hair with his free hand. "I'll always love you for this, Henrietta."

She closed her eyes when he kissed her. He kissed her again on both cheeks, on her eyelids, and on the warm hollow at the back of her neck. Then he held her away from him a little and looked down at her.

"I never noticed it before," he said at last. "Maybe it's the excitement of tonight or maybe you've got an odd body chemistry or something. You seem to me so . . . so spicey."

"I don't know what you mean, Dallas."

"I can't explain it exactly," he said, "but when I kissed you just now, you tasted like a Lifesaver."

She hugged him quickly and put her face tight against his bare chest so no sound could escape. If she explained, she knew he would laugh and she would want to laugh with him.

But she did not want to laugh or even think about mint leaves, at least until tomorrow.

Chapter
14

Next morning, when she told her mother and brother about the new foal and her ride to find Dr. Meacham, Two touched her arm and said, "That Dallas is some kind of guy. I ought to bicycle out and ask for his autograph or something."

"I'll drive you out," Retta said. "Maybe tomorrow. And you, too, Mother. Dallas wants you to see Estrellita."

"As soon as your father gets back," Mrs. Caldwell said. "I'll be less tied up at the paper then."

"Where is Poppy this time?" Retta asked. "He seems to be away as much as he's home these days."

"He's in Zenith again," her mother said.

"That's the third or fourth time in the last six weeks," Two said.

"Why is he doing this?" Retta asked. "When that highway ruined our farm, I thought he'd never want to see the countryside again."

Mrs. Caldwell began to break up the leftover breakfast toast for the desert birds. "This trip has nothing to do with the farm," she said. "That's over. Your father had some important business back in Pennsylvania. He had to consult with lawyers and others. It involves a lot of money and some difficult decisions."

"You make it all sound so mysterious," Retta said.

Her mother smiled, but her face was sad. "He'll tell us about it when the time is right. Your father likes to be sure about things."

When Retta drove to the ranch that evening, the first person she saw was Mrs. Bradley standing alone in the corral, currying Estrella's coat. The new foal was gamboling between the mare's legs.

"Come see our little one, Retta," Mrs. Bradley called out. "She's getting stronger by the hour. Dr. Meacham says she'll be on alfalfa hay by the end of next month."

Retta climbed the fence and hunkered down, calling softly to the foal. She came to her at once, nuzzling her upturned palm with a nose like warm velvet.

"We flew back from Scottsdale this morning," Mrs. Bradley said. "Thank goodness both of these animals are in perfect shape.

"I can't tell you how grateful we are to you both, Henrietta," she went on. Then she laughed. "I've been trying to say that to Dallas all day, and to tell him how pleased we've been with his work these past months. But you know how your boyfriend is. He gets embarrassed by praise and runs off to find some chore to do."

"I'll tell him what you said, Mrs. Bradley. Where is he now?"

The woman nodded toward the barn. "He and my husband are going over accounts. We've become so accustomed to having Dallas around, I'd almost begun to hope that — "

Retta shook her head. "He's definite about going back."

"Yes, we know that. He told us this morning about the scholarship and his other plans," Mrs. Bradley said gently. "He can be proud of that, too." Retta nodded without speaking.

"But you, Retta, Dallas tells me you'll be going to the new high school. Won't we see something of you from time to time? Perhaps you could come out for a canter with me. Evenings are lovely here in autumn. Or better still," she said, her voice bright with a new idea, "why not drive out every once in a while to take photographs of Estrellita? We've decided to keep that beautiful name, by the way. You and I could make a running scrapbook together to mail to Dallas. He could see how our baby is growing. Could you do that?"

"Thank you, Mrs. Bradley," she said. "Let me think about it."

The woman studied her for a moment. "Retta," she began, "I would like to say something to you. I'm sorry now that I wasn't more hospitable at the beginning of the summer, and that I objected to your coming out in the early mornings. I didn't really know either of you well and — "

"It doesn't matter, ma'am, not now. I'd forgotten all about it."

"Really? I wonder if you have," Mrs. Bradley said.

In the next few moments of silence, Retta became aware once again of the magic of this place, the shifts in evening shadows out beyond the fences, the brilliance of the fading sunset. As always for her, there was the uplifting, spiritual feeling of endless space at Rancho Arabian, earth and sky, reaching out to something unseen and unknown beyond.

Yet this stretch of bleakly beautiful desert could no longer be a part of her life, she knew. Without Dallas Dobson as the living, vital figure at the center of this beloved landscape, it would be impossible for her ever again to drive out to this place.

As if reading those thoughts, Mrs. Bradley said, "Perhaps he could arrange to fly back during the Christmas holidays. We could put him up here. Isn't that a possibility?"

"It's not that," Retta said. "We have room at our house, thank you. But Dallas has to work hard in Pennsylvania. Even with a scholarship, he'll need money to stay in college. And he helps out with his father. Dallas just can't *afford* things."

"Of course," Mrs. Bradley said apologetically. "From coast to coast, it's more than a three-thousand-mile trip. I should have remembered that."

Without planning to, without putting it into words, they began to do things together for the last time.

One evening, they drove out to the Bunking Bronco and sat in the booth they had occupied the first night. When the bartender brought their soft drinks, he said, "Tonight's on the house, cowboy. Chico Gomez says you're going back to school. Good luck. You did fine in our neck of the woods."

On another date, after chores, they went to the lab in the barn to straighten shelves and allow Dallas to leaf through the medical books for the last time. They worked for nearly two hours, with Dallas pausing frequently to reread pages, careful to take out wisps of straw he had used as bookmarks.

One blazing afternoon, air-conditioning on high, Retta and Dallas took her car into Thirty-nine Palms to purchase supplies for restocking both the tack room and birthing facility. Then, in a luggage shop in the mall, Dallas selected a sturdy new canvas suitcase, dark green with black straps.

On a particularly windless, sultry evening, they agreed to do nothing at all except drive the yellow car just outside the ranch gates and park in the sheltered lee of the high, thick hedge of tamarisk trees.

Dallas opened the sunroof to tepid night air and a desert sky, distant but pricked with brilliant stars. He turned the radio low to country music and they sat for hours, hands touching, heads leaning back on the car seats so they could look up into the twinkling darkness, peaceful, with almost no need for words.

"I'd like to send you those Duke Ellington tapes," Dallas said once, breaking the silence. "The ones we played when you drove me to school back east. They belonged to Sam Houston, you know. I'll look around for them as soon as I get home."

185

"Home?" she asked. "Back to Snuff Mill Road? That means you've finally talked to your father, doesn't it?"

"Yes," he said. "I called him yesterday. He expects me."

"You really feel you can live with him again?"

"At least I have to try."

"And is he going to meet you at the airport?"

"No, Mr. Engel will do that. I called him Monday to apologize for taking so long to reply and to be sure the scholarship deal is still on. It is. He said he and his wife would come to pick me up in Philadelphia. Mr. Engel sounded excited."

"Did your dad sound excited?"

Dallas was thoughtful. "Not really. He sounded like there was someone else in the house. You know how my father is. He likes to have a woman friend around."

"What *did* you talk about?"

"Not much, really. A little about the weather back home, the fact that I'd be there soon. I didn't tell him anything about the scholarship or much about this summer."

"Did you tell him about Estrellita?"

"No," he said. "I want to be home a few hours before I do that. We have to talk about *him* first. I want to be able to watch his face when I tell him about the foaling."

Dallas's return ticket was dated for September third, the following Sunday, at noon.

By late Wednesday afternoon, Carter Caldwell had still not left Pennsylvania and it was Mrs. Caldwell's suggestion that the three of them drive out to the ranch to see Estrellita, then ask if they could borrow Dallas for an early supper. Retta drove to a Mexican restaurant for some take-out food.

After a light supper in the cool dining room, Retta's mother said, "You'll all have to excuse me. I'm going to take a nap right now, even *before* I go to bed for the night. It's been a hot day, and a busy one. Plus the fact that your father's phone call woke me early this morning."

"The phone woke me, also," Two Caldwell said. "Why doesn't Poppy come home to talk with you instead of calling all the time?"

"He's coming soon," she answered. "Not tonight, but tomorrow for sure."

"I hope I have a chance to say good-bye," Dallas said.

"Oh, yes," Mrs. Caldwell told him. "He definitely wants to talk with you before you fly out."

Together, they put the supper dishes in the dishwasher. Then Dallas said, "If you drive me back now, I can still help out. The regular man won't be back from Europe till Monday. Those chores are a lot for the Bradleys to handle."

In the ranch driveway, he stood by the open car door. "I've been thinking, Retta. I don't want Friday and Saturday to be the last nights. What I mean to say is that I'll be packing then, and the Bradleys will be there. We can't be alone. Let's make tomorrow, Thursday, the last night for us."

"The Bradleys will be at the ranch tomorrow. How can we be alone?"

"I'll get permission to saddle up a couple of horses after chores. We'll ride up to where I worked out with Arista. It's private. We can be gone as long as we want. I'd like you to see the place at night, Retta, all stars and shadows. It's like escaping to moon country."

"But just one favor, Dallas."

"Anything."

"Don't mention anymore that it's almost our last night."

At home that evening, Retta found a note in her mother's handwriting pinned to her pillow. "Charlotte A. phoned. Call her back as soon as you can."

She looked at the bedside clock. It was half past eleven, which meant it was nearly two-thirty in the morning in Pennsylvania.

Retta tiptoed out into the hall, saw a light under her mother's door, and knocked. Mrs. Caldwell was in bed, propped up with pillows, a book held loosely in her hands.

"I hope I didn't wake you, Mother."

"No. I guess I was half dozing, half reading."

"I don't understand this note. You mean I'm supposed to call Charlotte *now?*"

"She said 'as soon as you can.' That's an odd household. Charlie and her mother keep strange hours. I'd call now if I were you, Retta."

"When did she phone?"

"About four-thirty, when you were out getting dinner. Your brother apologizes. He was so excited about going to the ranch, he forgot to give you the message."

"I'll call her, then," Retta said. "By the way, Mother, I'll be out late tomorrow. Dallas asked me to come about ten in the evening for a last ride in the desert. Is that all right with you?"

Her mother nodded. "I expect to pick up your father at the airport in the afternoon. We can have a family evening together here before you meet Dallas."

In the front foyer, Retta dialed the Amberson number, but strangely, the phone in the faraway Pennsylvania house did not ring. Instead, an operator's recorded voice came on the line, repeated the number Retta had dialed, then announced, "The number you are calling has been disconnected. There is no new listed number." The message was repeated a second time.

Puzzled, she hung up the phone and went into the hallway, but the light no longer shone from under her mother's door. There was no one to talk with.

Retta stood alone in the darkness for several minutes, unwilling to go to bed, unable to face the long silence of the night alone. She felt a heavy sensation in her heart, a growing anxiety close to fear. The truth of the upcoming separation from Dallas seemed to crowd closer with every breath.

But even this deep concern with her own feelings could not keep out a second persistent apprehension. Something unusual had happened at the Ambersons'.

Next morning, from the newspaper office, Mrs. Caldwell tried the Amberson number and got the same "No new listed number" recording.

"Let's not worry about them now," she said to Retta, seated at an adjoining desk. "I'm sure your father will have news."

Three times that Thursday morning, Mrs. Caldwell

took long distance calls from her husband. On the final call, Retta heard her say, "I've got that, Carter. United Flight Two Fifty-Seven, getting in at five-thirty. I'll be there."

"Do you want me to do anything special at home while you're picking up Poppy?" Retta asked.

"Please," her mother said. "Set the table for four. Unthaw small steaks, make a green salad. And look in the wine rack for a bottle of Mouton-Cadet. I know he'll want a glass of wine."

At four-thirty, Mrs. Caldwell phoned the airport to check if United Flight 257 from Philadelphia was on time. She made notes as she listened.

"Oh, dear," she said to Retta at the end of the call. "That flight *did* arrive at the O'Hare stopover in Chicago on time, but now takeoff is delayed. There are severe electrical storms over Lake Michigan."

"I guess Poppy won't like that," Retta said.

"I'm the one who worries most," Mrs. Caldwell answered, moving to close the drawers and stack papers on her desk. "I might as well go to the airport and do my worrying there. We'll be home just as soon as we can."

"You do remember, don't you," Retta said carefully, "that I have a date with Dallas at ten tonight?"

Her mother was thoughtful for a moment. "We'll surely be home long before that. Just keep your date, Henrietta."

Retta was already in the garage at half past nine, car keys in hand, when she heard the phone. She rushed back into the house to lift the receiver on the fifth ring.

190

"Caldwell residence," she said quickly, trying to catch her breath. "This is Henrietta."

"I *know* it's Henrietta," a sharp voice said. "I'm calling from the airport."

"Good, Pops. You're home. Mother is around there somewhere looking for you. . . ."

"Your mother is standing right beside me, Henrietta. It's *you* I want to talk with."

"All right. I'm listening."

"That's not what I mean. I want you where I can talk with you face-to-face. Your mother tells me you planned a date tonight. I'm sorry, but you'll have to cancel. I want you right there, and your brother also, when we get home from the airport."

"Oh, you can't do this, Poppy!" Retta burst out. "You and I've got a whole lifetime. But with Dallas — there's just two more days. Please don't tell me not to see him."

"Retta," her father said firmly, "I want to talk with you *tonight* — about one of the most important things that has ever happened to our family. It is either a blessing or a tragedy, your mother and I aren't sure which."

"You sound strange, Poppy. What is it? You're making me feel frightened. How long will this talk take?"

"It could be an hour, it could take all night." His voice softened. "You won't be frightened when I explain everything to you. Just *be there*, Henrietta."

"All right, Poppy," she said sadly. "I'll call Dallas."

"That's my good girl."

When Retta dialed Rancho Arabian, Mrs. Bradley answered and agreed to deliver the message. "Let's see if I have it," she said. "Your father just got back from Pennsylvania. He called you from the airport. Something important has come up and he must talk with you. You can't go riding tonight with Dallas as planned but will call him later. . . ."

"That's it, and thank you."

"I'll walk out to the stables to tell him," the older woman said. "He asked me earlier about taking out a pair of mounts and I said fine. I'm afraid he's going to be disappointed."

"No more disappointed than I am, Mrs. Bradley."

It seemed impossible to wait sitting still, so Retta got into her car to cruise around the neighborhood. After circling several blocks, she found Two with some other boys shooting baskets into a garage-door hoop. As they drove home, she told her brother about the phone call.

"You've got me worried," he said. "I feel awful, in fact. What's this all about?"

Retta shook her head. "You just wash up and get into something neat," she instructed him. "It's important that Poppy *like* us both tonight."

Back home, she cleared away the unused dinner things, put on a pot of coffee, and set out a tray with wine glasses, cups, and saucers. As the percolator hiccuped, the sound loud in the quiet house, Henrietta went into her own bathroom.

Her image in the mirror looked almost unfamiliar to her. An hour before, getting ready to meet Dallas, her face had been soft, flushed, expectant. Now, under a summer tan, there was a paleness, a white tension that seemed to circle her eyes and stretch taut over her worried forehead.

One of the most important things that has hap-

pened in our lives, her father had said. *Either a tragedy or a blessing . . .*

"Please!" she murmured aloud. "Dear God, I'm begging You. Don't make it either. Let my father tell me something *ordinary* tonight. Let him — "

At that moment, the family car turned into the driveway with a screech of tires. Retta switched off the light above the mirror and went to greet her parents, leaving the prayer unfinished.

Chapter
15

Carter Caldwell pulled his chair into the circle of light at the dining table and waited while his wife poured two glasses of wine. Then he put an attaché case in front of him and removed a thick envelope. From that he extracted a large sheet of blue surveyor's paper with white ink markings and smoothed it out on the table.

"I wonder, Two, if either you or your sister know what this is," he said.

Two pulled the paper closer to him and squinted down at it. "It's like a map, I think. Those lines could be roads and maybe those little crisscrosses are trees or bushes. But the writing goes every which way," he said.

"Those double curving lines, that must be the two-lane black road that Retta used to take to school," he went on. "Because these little block shapes here are marked 'Kennelly' and that's the farm where Dallas worked, where she'd pick him up. I mean, the house and the barn. This stretch of crosses, that's their woods."

Two pointed and moved the blue paper closer to his sister. "Right, Retta?"

Retta touched the paper lightly with one finger and pushed it nearer to the center of the table. "Do we have to have guessing games, Poppy? Especially tonight?" she asked. "Why don't you tell us what this is?"

"It's a surveyor's map," Mr. Caldwell said. "It covers some property I think you're familiar with."

Two leaned forward to peer more closely at the big sketch. "It can't be our old farm because there's no six-lane highway showing anywhere." He pointed to some printing on the paper. "Yet here is a line marked 'Willow Road.' That was the north boundary to our place, way over at the edge and not far from the house where Aunt Blue used to live. Am I right about that?"

His father nodded. "What else do you recognize?"

"Well, a little bit of everything, and not anything, really. I can see from the north and south markings, and by the side roads, that this sketch also covers those woods and meadow where nobody lived. Isn't this that big, beautiful stretch of country right behind Aunt Blue's little place?"

Mr. Caldwell nodded, then put his finger on a small rectangle, marked with windows and a chimney, almost in the exact center of the map. "And what's this?" he asked.

Retta pulled the big sheet directly in front of her and studied it carefully. "That has to be Aunt Blue's house. And the two smaller buildings are her chicken coop and the old toolshed she used for a garage."

Her voice quickened with emotion. "It's not really marked, but here is where she kept the garden she was so proud of." Retta pointed. "And right here would be those four pear trees. Every autumn Aunt Blue cooked up that great pear chutney of hers, the kind she tinted with blue food coloring."

"We got gift jars of that chutney every Christmas," her mother said. "I'm glad you have such good memories, Retta. That could help . . ."

Even though Mrs. Caldwell was smiling, the voice seemed sad. Retta noticed for the first time her mother's reddened eyes, the dash of powder around the nose. Some time not long ago, she knew — and perhaps even on the way home from the airport — her mother had been crying.

"Poppy, please," Retta said quietly. "On the phone you said this was one of the most important things to happen in our lives. That worries me. I can tell Mother's upset, too. Can't you explain? All I see on this surveyor's sketch is Aunt Blue's house and yard, and around them those big hunks of woods and meadows you could see from her house."

"Do you remember much about that land?"

"Of course I do," Retta said. "Aunt Blue used to take Two and me walking on that property, espe- cially in the springtime. It was wild country, like no human had ever lived or farmed there; just a natural, untouched place. Aunt Blue always called it God's

196

Own Acres. She sort of looked after it. I never knew who owned that land."

Her father reached over to cover his wife's slender hand with his large one. Then he said, "I wanted you to hear this altogether, as a family, because it affects all of us. That surveyor's map is what my recent trips back to Zenith have been all about.

"As you know," he went on, "I was named an executor of Aunt Blue's estate. Ever since she died, we've been trying to put her property in order. For months and months, I've been checking with lawyers, the courthouse, her church, the state office of deed and registry — everything I could think of — that might give us information. We weren't making much headway because we believed she had died intestate."

"That means without leaving a will," Two said.

"Anyway," Mr. Caldwell went on, "about six weeks ago, a will *did* turn up in Gethsemane, Kentucky. Aunt Blue had left it at the convent with a friend, someone she'd known at the orphanage a long time ago. But that friend was an elderly nun, getting on in years. She completely forgot she had the will until she ran across it in her desk one day. Mother Superior phoned me at once."

Mr. Caldwell took a sip of wine. "Since then, I've gone over the document a dozen times. A team of Zenith lawyers also checked to see that there were no errors, no false hopes or promises. We are now sure of our facts.

"Retta," he said, "a few moments ago, you said you never knew who owned God's Own Acres." He paused, as if hesitant to say the next words, so important, so final. "Now we know.

"All the land shown on this map, north and south, from Willow Road right up to the Kennelly's fence line, was purchased and legally registered in the name of Mrs. Paula Saint-Scales, our Aunt Blue. Mrs. Saint-Scales owned the property outright. And now, Henrietta, it belongs to you. All of it."

"*What* belongs to me?" Retta asked, her voice high with surprise. "Why do you say 'all of it'? All of *what*, Poppy? I don't understand. Aunt Blue owned nothing but a brick house and a little yard. . . ."

Her father shook his head. "We didn't know as much about Mrs. Saint-Scales as we thought we did, Retta. She was eighty-six years old that morning when you found her peacefully dead in her bed. Until we read the will, and the dates, we had no idea she was that old. She had worked all her life in other people's houses. She was proud. We *did* know that."

Retta felt a sudden need to cry. "I was so sad when she died. She taught me so much — even how to make those pies with designs on them."

"Aunt Blue had been widowed years ago," Carter Caldwell went on. "There were no children, no living relatives. All through her working life, for nearly sixty years, she had been buying up bits and pieces of land around her house — an acre here, two acres there — until she owned three hundred acres, all in one piece."

Mrs. Caldwell poured a cup of coffee and held her hand over it as if to warm her fingers in the steam.

"Everything your father is telling you, he told to me as it developed," she said. "I promised not to

198

say anything till every legal angle had been checked. The check is over. We know now the bequests are final and legal.

"Aunt Blue's will gives Two an inheritance of five thousand dollars the day he turns eighteen and another five thousand the day if and when, he is graduated from college," Mrs. Caldwell said. "Aunt Blue also wanted him to have her guitars and clock collection. Otherwise, Retta, you are her sole heir. You own the house, the furniture, the yard, the pear trees — and all of God's Own Acres."

"But why?" Retta asked. "Why *me?*"

"That will was drawn up some years ago," her father explained. "It was dated the day after you discovered the red flags and stakes that marked where the highway would go through our property. That was the first time we realized we were going to get a six-laner. Do you remember that?"

"Yes," Henrietta said. "I was fourteen, I think. So angry, so hurt. And then, Poppy, you told me, 'Laws are made by people and laws must be obeyed by people.' That didn't make it any better, so I went over to Aunt Blue's house to cry. But why are we talking this way?" she asked suddenly. "What can I do with a house and land three thousand miles away from my *home?* Can't I just sell everything and put the money away for college? Or couldn't we all take a big trip together, fly to Paris or Hawaii?"

"Aunt Blue expected you to keep her bequest, at least for a while," her father said.

"Then I've just come up with a great idea," Retta said, her voice tense with excitement. "Why don't we *all go back* and live at Aunt Blue's place? We can sell off some of the land and add onto the house — more bedrooms, a new kitchen. The Caldwells could start over again in Pennsylvania."

Two's voice was puzzled when he spoke. "Go *back*, Retta? I thought we all *liked* California. I have new friends here and I never thought I'd get such a great tan. . . ."

"Your brother is speaking for himself," Mr. Caldwell said. "I believe I can speak for your mother and me, Retta. We've made a commitment here, the newspaper, the new printing plant. We're like pioneers who came west to start a fresh life. We're beginning to *belong* in California."

"I *also* made the trip west," Retta said. "I've even registered at a new school. Can't we go on with our lives? Can't we leave this inheritance alone? Forget about it?"

"I'm afraid not, Retta," Mr. Caldwell said. "And please listen carefully so you understand what we're saying as *parents*. Aunt Blue never meant to break up a family, your mother and I are sure of that. Yet she never expected to die suddenly in the night as she did, even at eighty-six years of age. She undoubtedly hoped you'd be grown and into a life of your own before you became her heir. But — " He looked over at his wife.

"But *what*, Poppy?" Henrietta asked urgently.

"No matter how we feel, we have no choice in this matter. . . ."

"But *what*, Poppy?" she asked again, gently this time.

"According to law, you — Henrietta Caldwell — as legal heir, must be told of your inheritance and all your legal rights in regard to it. If you should, for any reason, refuse the terms of the will, Aunt

Blue's bequest will go directly to the convent in Gethsemane, Kentucky, where she lived as a child.

"If, as parents, we *didn't* inform you of these matters, then Mr. Hoopes in Zenith, as second executor, would be obliged to act in your behalf. He would give you the same information I've given you, and more."

"More? There's something *more* you have to tell me?" Retta asked, her voice now tremulous.

"Yes," her father said. "A special clause in the will says you must live in Aunt Blue's house for two consecutive years. Aunt Blue stated that she wants to be sure you understand and love God's Own Acres. At the end of two years, the property is yours to do with as you wish. You might even decide to move back to California."

"I could never *afford* to live there," Retta protested. "I have to finish school. I can't get a job to earn upkeep for a house all by myself."

"Aunt Blue thought of that," her father said. "There is some money in her safe-deposit box in the bank that goes to you the day you move in. That means, Retta, that you would have enough to run things for the next two years you'll be in school in Pennsylvania."

"Two years? I expect to be out of high school next June."

Her father seemed not to have heard. "And for the second year, you could commute from Aunt Blue's to that fine junior college in West Chester. And then — "

"How can you do this to me?" Henrietta said with a flash of deep anger. "You've got my whole life mapped out for me. You're literally *sending me*

201

away. I'll never be a real member of this family again. I'm not sure I can stand that."

"Please, Retta," her mother said. "You will always be a part of us, no matter where you are. Your happiness is of prime importance. Ever since I first heard this news, I've prayed your decision would be right for you. . . ."

"You mean I have some kind of *choice?* I can just turn the whole inheritance down if I want? The old place meant a lot to me in a special way when Aunt Blue was alive. But it can't be worth much, not really."

Her father shook his head. "You are wrong if you believe that property can't be worth much. And this is something else you are entitled to know under the law: the monetary value of your inheritance."

He put the surveyor's map in front of his daughter and drew the outlines of a large circle with the eraser tip of a pencil.

"Since the highway took so much prime acreage in that part of the state, the land of God's Own Acres — untouched as it is — is choice building real estate. Already there have been developers asking to buy it for countrystyle luxury homes."

"Even so, how much could it be worth?" Retta asked.

Her father opened his attaché case and took out a sheaf of papers lined with figures. "Clem Hoopes at the Zenith Bank had a value analysis done," he said. "You would own three hundred acres, Retta, with the possibility of selling half-acre lots, or six hundred land parcels at the average price of ten thousand dollars a lot."

"Even I can figure that one out," Two said, and

gave a low whistle. "Retta, that comes to six hundred thousand dollars!"

"That's if you sold it as individual lots or packaged parcels," her father went on. "But Mr. Hoopes already has in his office safe a validated offer from a New York land developer who wants to take over your entire property — the full three hundred acres — for the round figure of eight hundred fifty thousand dollars. That's based on current land prices. As time passes, the value of the property can only go up."

"That's a lot of money, I know," Retta said. "But I don't think Aunt Blue would like God's Own Acres broken up with a lot of houses."

"Nothing in the will tells us what Aunt Blue thought about subdividing," her father said.

"She didn't have to put it in writing," Retta said. "I think she'd trust me to *remember* what she liked. Aunt Blue liked natural, outdoor, open things. Not cement roads and high fences." Retta studied the map and traced her finger around the outlines of God's Own Acres.

"I've got an important question, Poppy. If I *don't* accept the terms of the will, and the inheritance *does* go to the religious community in Kentucky, what do *they* plan to do with Aunt Blue's land?"

"Mr. Hoopes checked the good nuns out on that. They plan to sell the entire property at once to the highest-bidding land developer to build on as he chooses. That particular religious community needs cash."

"I know what Aunt Blue would want, but my whole life will change. I won't be *myself* anymore," Retta said sadly.

"Of course you will," her mother broke in. "We can write every day, call as often as we like. You can fly here for Christmas and Two can spend summers with you.

"I can bear the thought of this separation, Retta, only because in Zenith, you'll be with friends, old Mrs. Curtayne, the Ambersons, teachers at school, Junior Provanza and his sister. Dozens of people who know you and love you. You won't be alone."

Retta's head had begun to ache and she seemed to hear her mother talking as if in a dream. In the unreality of this strange evening, she had almost forgotten Dallas.

Now, at the thought of him, she stood up so quickly she almost tipped the chair backward. "The most important person who'll be back there — *aren't you forgetting him?*"

"No, we're not," her father said. "We are all aware that Dallas is flying home on Sunday. We didn't forget that for a minute."

"It will be almost like it was, only different, won't it?" Retta said. "He'll be a full senior and we'll be going to the same school, for a semester at least. We'll see each other every day. He's going to live with his father again . . . if he can. He has to sleep on a couch in that house. There's no real place to study. . . . And me — suddenly I have money and an empty house with lots of room. I wouldn't *have* to live alone, would I? Dallas could move in. We could really be together in the way he wants. Didn't you think of that? Is that what you expect of us? It would be so easy. . . ."

"No, Henrietta," her father said without heat.

"That is *not* what we expect of you, or Dallas, either. Your mother and I didn't intend to leave such an important decision up to you alone." He paused. "We've found someone to share Aunt Blue's home with you, at least for the crucial two years."

"I can't live with strangers," Retta said.

"Not strangers," Carter Caldwell said. "Charlie Amberson and her mother are flat broke. They were forced to give up their home. Since last week, they've been living in a motel. I had a long talk with the Ambersons two days ago, suggesting they share Aunt Blue's house, if you agree. Young Charlie is delighted but Charlotte, Sr., was a bit of a problem. She said she couldn't take charity. I explained that she'd be paid as housekeeper and companion, to keep an eye on you young ladies."

"I can't have you and Mother paying for someone to look after me," Retta said. "I'm a little old for a live-in babysitter."

"*You* would be paying Mrs. Amberson, Retta. Charlotte Amberson's salary will come from you. And so will the other checks and decisions about running that household," Mr. Caldwell said.

"I really get to decide things?" Retta asked. "I can make plans, spend money, write out checks?" Her father nodded.

"I want to be clear about certain conditions," Retta went on. "I *must* live in the house for two years, but I won't have to change anything at all, is that right? I don't have to give up one piece of furniture, one harmonica, one old Bible. . . . And I don't have to build one fence or cut down one tree in the whole three hundred acres if I don't want to?"

"That's how the lawyers, Mr. Hoopes, and I interpret Aunt Blue's wishes," her father answered gravely. "At God's Own Acres, you are in charge."

Retta sat down in silence. She knew her parents were waiting for her to speak, but her head was spinning with splintered thoughts and unasked questions.

"When would all this happen?" she asked finally.

"That's up to you," her father said. "But Havendale High does start the fall semester next Tuesday."

At that moment, the front doorbell rang, one long, shrill ring, as if someone had pressed an insistent finger on the buzzer.

"Oh, dear," Mrs. Caldwell said. "Were we talking too loudly? Could that be one of the neighbors? What time is it anyway?"

"It's after midnight," her husband said. "Let me check the door."

From the front foyer came a murmur of greetings and then Dallas's voice sounded clear and strong in the silent house.

"Retta said she'd call me but she didn't, Mr. Caldwell. That's not like her. If there's something wrong, I want to be with her."

"I'm glad you're here, Dallas," they heard Mr. Caldwell say. "I had planned to talk with you, tell you certain things before you left. But business back East tied me up."

In the dining area, Dallas shook hands with both Mrs. Caldwell and Two. Carter Caldwell signaled for him to take a seat at the table.

"I'll just stand, sir," Dallas said, and positioned

himself behind Retta's chair, both hands on her shoulders.

"Shall I explain what we've been discussing, Retta?" her father asked. "Or would you rather do it yourself?"

"You do it, Poppy," she said. She turned in her chair to look up at Dallas. "I should warn you, you're going to be surprised. You may not even like the news. I'm not sure I do." She paused. "Just listen for now, Dallas. Please. Don't even tell me what you think. I can't decide anything tonight anyway. It's all too big. It changes too much. As Aunt Blue would say, 'This child needs to *sleep* on it.' "

She looked at her father. "Go ahead, Poppy. Tell him everything."

Over the Caldwell garden, the night sky had begun to fade into a new day before everything was said that had to be said. Two was asleep, his head on his arms. The sheets of figures and blue surveyors' maps had finally been folded back into the attaché case. Mrs. Caldwell brought in a last pot of coffee. Retta noticed that under the overhead lights, her father's dark hair was touched with gray, his face tired and pensive.

"Is that all then, Poppy?" she asked gently. Dallas's hands were warm on her shoulders and she could feel the welcome strength of his fingers as he pressed into the taut muscles of her neck. With a sigh, she leaned back against him.

"That's all we need to talk about," Mr. Caldwell answered. "At least until you've come to a decision on this, Retta."

But there was one more thing that needed to be said, and Retta turned again to look at Dallas as she spoke.

"I just want you to know something, Dallas. It's important to both of us. No matter what is decided, no matter what happens in the next two years, nothing will make me turn into somebody else."

Chapter
16

There were not enough hours left to make it a long night. Nor was Retta distinctly aware of lying awake, sleeping, or even of falling in and out of dreams.

Her thinking processes seemed accelerated but involuntary. It was as if all the news of the previous evening had come alive in her mind like a series of quick, visual movie scenes, moving through her consciousness, acted out by familiar characters, speaking familiar dialogue.

In this night of decision, she was aware of many important things she had known and loved: Aunt Blue with her kindness and strange wisdom; the lifelong trust and comfort of two parents; memory glimpses of trees and birds; that wild green stretch of Pennsylvania called God's Own Acres.

She recalled with the original happiness that magic moment of seeing Two in the hospital, a pink and squawling infant, her first and only brother. All the cats and dogs she had ever owned began a slow parade through her mind. She thought of the two Ambersons in their vine-covered brick house; the new foal, Estrellita, wobbly in the bright sunlight; the long red dress she had worn to the prom; the western jeans with stitching she had bought in the mall.

Suddenly she could see clearly in her mind's eye every worn, old classroom at Havendale High, and even the new library at Thirty-nine Palms, smelling of fresh varnish, empty shelves waiting for books. There were past Christmases to remember, snow on old roofs, pink lilacs in the springtime, and letters from her grandmother in Florida, each containing a pressed and perfumed five-dollar bill. There was the comforting sound of her mother making early morning coffee in the kitchen at the farm. And the strange, wonderful day when the new person, the Texas cowboy, had come into her math class and into her life. . . .

With no real effort on her part, Retta's mind switched off the past and turned to scenes of the future, a murky but challenging scenario of what might lie ahead.

Her parents were in some of those scenes, the Ambersons, brother Two, and Mr. Engel. And there were many others, new people who said little and — as yet — had no filled-in faces.

210

Slowly but inevitably, Retta became aware of the constant presence of one special person, and the reality of that fact brought her abruptly and widely awake.

In the center of most of those new dreams, sometimes alone, sometimes with her (or, if she were alone, his shadow fell nearby), but there, always there, was Dallas Dobson.

It was barely dawn when she let her car drift backward down the slanting driveway to the street. Then, as quietly as she could, she switched on the motor and drove off down Desert Lily.

Near Rancho Arabian, almost abreast of the tamarisk trees, she rolled down the car window. She breathed deeply, wanting to slow the rapid pace of her heartbeat and needing once more to inhale the familiar, reassuring scents of dust-dry creosote, sage blossoms, and the almost crystalline fragrance of warm sand.

A short distance from the Bradley driveway, she pulled to the side of the road, then walked to the gate with light footsteps. As she opened it, the black iron hinges sounded out with a sharp, metallic creak.

Retta paused, aware of the silent big house, the sleeping Bradleys. I must tell Dallas, she thought. He has almost three days left here. Those hinges need oil.

The double barn door had been unlocked and thrown open to the morning air, and she knew that in a few moments, she could find him there.

A feeling of pure joy touched her spirit, so powerful, so acute that it felt almost like pain. Retta stopped suddenly, took a deep breath, and called out Dallas's name, waiting as she heard it echo out toward the mountains.

It no longer seemed important whether or not the Bradleys might hear her. She almost wanted them to. She had made her decision and she felt sure he would agree with her. She and Dallas could now reclaim their morning together, today for sure, and then — perhaps — for a lifetime.

She called out his name again and waited till he hurried from the barn, looking about him, squinting into the morning sunlight. When he raised a hand in greeting, she ran to where he was.

"The Bradley gate needs oiling, Dallas," she said quickly. "It has a bad squeak. And I think you'd better check out the one in Pennsylvania with me, next week maybe. It hasn't been used in a long time." She touched his hand tenderly with hers as she spoke.

She had said it. With those spare, oblique words she had let him know just how deeply she felt about Dallas Dobson.

All of God's Own Acres was her property now, even the old front gate. Six or eight weathered slats, a hasp lock, and a pair of antique hinges that had hung there for years, but an important gate. It gave her choices.

She could choose to close and lock it, she knew, or she was free to swing it open wide, night or day, to welcome anyone she would need in her new life.

"I know you've never been to Aunt Blue's house, Dallas," Retta said quietly. "The gate has a little bell

212

on it that you have to ring to be let in."

When he looked puzzled, she added, "But you won't have to bother to ring the bell. The house is on an old back-country road. No matter what time it is, I'll hear you coming. I'm sure I will."